A Collection of Cl

MW00613468

Mark Twain
Oscar Wilde
Sir Arthur Conan Doyle
Saki
Jack London

***Edited by* Yona Rodrigue Cohen**

A Collection of Classic Short Stories

Published by
ELL Reading, LLC
P.O. Box 1137
Mason, OH 45040, USA

Library of Congress Control Number: 2010927503

ISBN: 978-0-9844098-1-5

Printed in United States of America

Table of Contents

The £1,000,000 Bank-Note

N/MC = [illegible]
1st POV Henry

When I was twenty-seven years old, I was a mining-broker's clerk in San Francisco, and an expert in all the details of stock traffic. I was alone in the world, and had nothing to depend upon but my wits and a clean reputation; but these were setting my feet in the road to eventual fortune, and I was content with the **prospect**.

My time was my own after the afternoon board, Saturdays, and I was accustomed to put it in on a little sail-boat on the bay. One day I **ventured** too far, and was carried out to sea. Just at nightfall, when hope was about gone, I was picked up by a small brig which was bound for London. It was a long and stormy voyage, and they made me work my passage without pay, as a common sailor. When I stepped ashore in London my clothes were ragged and shabby, and I had only a dollar in my pocket. This money fed and sheltered me twenty-four hours. During the next twenty-four I went without food and shelter.

About ten o'clock on the following morning, seedy and hungry, I was dragging myself along Portland Place, when a child that was passing, towed by a nurse-maid, tossed a **luscious**

---

prospect: expectation; promise
ventured: had the courage to go
luscious: tasty; sweet

big pear - minus one bite - into the gutter. I stopped, of course, and fastened my desiring eye on that muddy treasure. My mouth watered for it, my stomach craved it, my whole being begged for it. But every time I made a move to get it some passing eye detected my purpose, and of course I straightened up then, and looked indifferent, and pretended that I hadn't been thinking about the pear at all. This same thing kept happening and happening, and I couldn't get the pear. I was just getting desperate enough to brave all the shame, and to seize it, when a window behind me was raised, and a gentleman spoke out of it, saying:

"Step in here, please."

I was admitted by a gorgeous flunkey, and shown into a **sumptuous** room where a couple of elderly gentlemen were sitting. They sent away the servant, and made me sit down. They had just finished their breakfast, and the sight of the remains of it almost overpowered me. I could hardly keep my wits together in the presence of that food, but as I was not asked to sample it, I had to bear my trouble as best I could.

Now, something had been happening there a little before, which I did not know anything about until a good many days afterward, but I will tell you about it now. Those two old brothers had been having a pretty hot argument a couple of days before, and had ended by agreeing to decide it by a bet, which is the English way of settling everything.

You will remember that the Bank of England once

---

sumptuous: magnificent

issued two notes of a million pounds each, to be used for a special purpose connected with some public transaction with a foreign country. For some reason or other only one of these had been used and canceled; the other still lay in the **vaults** of the Bank. Well, the brothers, chatting along, happened to get to wondering what might be the fate of a perfectly honest and intelligent stranger who should be turned adrift in London without a friend, and with no money but that million-pound bank-note, and no way to account for his being in possession of it. Brother A said he would starve to death; Brother B said he wouldn't. Brother A said he couldn't offer it at a bank or anywhere else, because he would be arrested on the spot. So they went on disputing till Brother B said he would bet twenty thousand pounds that the man would live thirty days, *anyway*, on that million, and keep out of jail, too. Brother A **took him up**. Brother B went down to the Bank and bought that note. Just like an Englishman, you see; pluck to the backbone. Then he dictated a letter, which one of his clerks wrote out in a beautiful round hand, and then the two brothers sat at the window a whole day watching for the right man to give it to.

They saw many honest faces go by that were not intelligent enough; many that were intelligent, but not honest enough; many that were both, but the possessors were not poor enough, or, if poor enough, were not strangers. There was always a defect, until I came along; but they agreed that I filled the bill all around;

---

vaults: cellars

took him up: accepted the bet

so they elected me **unanimously**, and there I was now waiting to know why I was called in. They began to ask questions about myself, and pretty soon they had my story. Finally they told me I would answer their purpose. I said I was sincerely glad, and asked what it was. Then one of them handed me an envelope, and said I would find the explanation inside. I was going to open it, but he said no; take it to my lodgings, and look it over carefully, and not be hasty or rash. I was puzzled, and wanted to discuss the matter a little further, but they didn't; so I took my leave, feeling hurt and insulted to be made the **butt** of what was apparently some kind of a practical joke, and yet obliged to put up with it, not being in circumstances to resent **affronts** from rich and strong folk.

I would have picked up the pear now and eaten it before all the world, but it was gone; so I had lost that by this unlucky business, and the thought of it did not soften my feeling toward those men. As soon as I was out of sight of that house I opened my envelope, and saw that it contained money! My opinion of those people changed, I can tell you! I lost not a moment, but shoved note and money into my vest pocket, and broke for the nearest cheap eating-house. Well, how I did eat! When at last I couldn't hold any more, I took out my money and unfolded it, took one glimpse and nearly fainted. Five millions of dollars! Why, it made my head swim.

---

unanimously: agreeing fully

butt: object; aim

affronts: offensive, disrespectful language or behavior

I must have sat there stunned and blinking at the note as much as a minute before I came rightly to myself again. The first thing I noticed, then, was the landlord. His eye was on the note, and he was petrified. He was worshiping, with all his body and soul, but he looked as if he couldn't stir hand or foot. I took my cue in a moment, and did the only rational thing there was to do. I reached the note toward him, and said, carelessly:

"Give me the change, please."

Then he was restored to his normal condition, and made a thousand apologies for not being able to break the bill, and I couldn't get him to touch it. He wanted to look at it, and keep on looking at it; he couldn't seem to get enough of it to **quench** the thirst of his eye, but he shrank from touching it as if it had been something too sacred for poor common clay to handle. I said:

"I am sorry if it is an inconvenience, but I must insist. Please change it. I haven't anything else."

But he said that wasn't any matter; he was quite willing to let the trifle stand over till another time. I said I might not be in his neighborhood again for a good while; but he said it was of no consequence, he could wait, and, moreover, I could have anything I wanted, any time I chose, and let the account run as long as I pleased. He said he hoped he wasn't afraid to trust as rich a gentleman as I was, merely because I was of a merry disposition, and chose to play larks on the public in the matter of dress. By this time another customer was entering, and the landlord hinted to me to put the monster out of sight; then he

---

quench: satisfy

bowed me all the way to the door, and I started straight for that house and those brothers, to correct the mistake which had been made before the police should hunt me up, and help me do it. I was pretty nervous; in fact, pretty badly frightened, though, of course, I was no way in fault; but I knew men well enough to know that when they find they've given a tramp a million-pound bill when they thought it was a one-pounder, they are in a frantic rage against *him* instead of quarreling with their own near-sightedness, as they ought. As I approached the house my excitement began to **abate**, for all was quiet there, which made me feel pretty sure the blunder was not discovered yet. I rang. The same servant appeared. I asked for those gentlemen.

"They are gone." This in the lofty, cold way of that fellow's tribe.

"Gone? Gone where?"

"On a journey."

"But whereabouts?"

"To the Continent, I think."

"The Continent?"

"Yes, sir."

"Which way – by what route?"

"I can't say, sir."

"When will they be back?"

"In a month, they said."

"A month! Oh, this is awful! Give me *some* sort of idea of how to get a word to them. It's of the last importance."

---

abate: decrease; become less

"I can't, indeed. I've no idea where they've gone, sir."

"Then I must see some member of the family."

"Family's away, too; been abroad months – in Egypt and India, I think."

"Man, there's been an immense mistake made. They'll be back before night. Will you tell them I've been here, and that I will keep coming till it's all made right, and they needn't be afraid?"

"I'll tell them, if they come back, but I am not expecting them. They said you would be here in an hour to make inquiries, but I must tell you it's all right, they'll be here on time and expect you."

So I had to give it up and go away. What a riddle it all was! I was like to lose my mind. They would be here "on time." What could that mean? Oh, the letter would explain, maybe. I had forgotten the letter; I got it out and read it. This is what it said:

"You are an intelligent and honest man, as one may see by your face. We conceive you to be poor and a stranger. Enclosed you will find a sum of money. It is lent to you for thirty days, without interest. Report at this house at the end of that time. I have a bet on you. If I win it you shall have any situation that is in my gift – any, that is, that you shall be able to prove yourself familiar with and **competent** to fill."

No signature, no address, no date.

Well, here was a coil to be in! You are posted on what had

---

competent: qualified

preceded all this, but I was not. It was just a deep, dark puzzle to me. I hadn't the least idea what the game was, nor whether harm was meant me or a kindness. I went into a park, and sat down to try to think it out, and to consider what I had best do.

At the end of an hour my reasonings had crystallized into this verdict.

Maybe those men mean me well, maybe they mean me ill; no way to decide that – let it go. They've got a game, or a scheme, or an experiment, of some kind on hand; no way to determine what it is – let it go. There's a bet on me; no way to find out what it is – let it go. That disposes of the indeterminable quantities; the remainder of the matter is **tangible**, solid, and may be classed and labeled with certainty. If I ask the Bank of England to place this bill to the credit of the man it belongs to, they'll do it, for they know him, although I don't; but they will ask me how I came in possession of it, and if I tell the truth, they'll put me in the asylum, naturally, and a lie will land me in jail. The same result would follow if I tried to bank the bill anywhere or to borrow money on it. I have got to carry this immense burden around until those men come back, whether I want to or not. It is useless to me, as useless as a handful of ashes, and yet I must take care of it, and watch over it, while I beg my living. I couldn't *give* it away, if I should try, for neither honest citizen nor highwayman would accept it or meddle with it for anything. Those brothers are safe. Even if I lose their bill, or

---

preceded: came before

tangible: definite

burn it, they are still safe, because they can stop payment, and the bank will make them whole; but meantime I've got to do a month's suffering without wages or profit - unless I help win that bet, whatever it may be, and get that situation that I am promised. I *should* like to get that; men of their sort have situations in their gift that are worth having.

I got to thinking a good deal about that situation. My hopes began to rise high. Without doubt the salary would be large. It would begin in a month; after that I should be all right. Pretty soon I was feeling first rate. By this time I was tramping the streets again. The sight of a tailor-shop gave me a sharp longing to shed my rags, and to clothe myself decently once more. Could I afford it? No; I had nothing in the world but a million pounds. So I forced myself to go on by. But soon I was drifting back again. The temptation **persecuted** me cruelly. I must have passed that shop back and forth six times during that manful struggle. At last I gave in; I had to. I asked if they had a misfit suit that had been thrown on their hands. The fellow I spoke to nodded his head toward another fellow, and gave me no answer. I went to the indicated fellow, and he indicated another fellow with his head, and no words. I went to him, and he said:

" 'Tend to you presently. "

I waited till he was done with what he was at, then he took me into a back room, and overhauled a pile of rejected suits, and selected the rattiest one for me. I put it on. It didn't fit, and wasn't in any way attractive, but it was new, and I was anxious to

---

persecuted: bothered

have it; so I didn't find any fault, but said, with some diffidence:

"It would be an accommodation to me if you could wait some days for the money. I haven't any small change about me."

The fellow worked up a most **sarcastic** expression of countenance, and said:

"Oh, you haven't? Well, of course, I didn't expect it. I'd only expect gentlemen like you to carry large change."

I was nettled, and said:

"My friend, you shouldn't judge a stranger always by the clothes he wears. I am quite able to pay for this suit; I simply didn't wish to put you to the trouble of changing a large note."

He modified his style a little at that, and said, though still with something of an air:

"I didn't mean any particular harm, but as long as **rebukes** are going, I might say it wasn't quite your affair to jump to the conclusion that we couldn't change any note that you might happen to be carrying around. On the contrary, we *can*."

I handed the note to him, and said:

"Oh, very well; I apologize."

He received it with a smile, one of those large smiles which goes all around over, and has folds in it, and wrinkles, and spirals, and looks like the place where you have thrown a brick in a pond; and then in the act of his taking a glimpse of the bill this smile froze solid, and turned yellow, and looked like those wavy, wormy spreads of lava which you find hardened on little

---

sarcastic: ironic; hurtful; mocking

rebukes: critical remarks

levels on the side of Vesuvius. I never before saw a smile caught like that, and **perpetuated**. The man stood there holding the bill, and looking like that, and the proprietor hustled up to see what was the matter, and said, briskly:

"Well, what's up? what's the trouble? what's wanting?"

I said: "There isn't any trouble. I'm waiting for my change."

"Come, come; get him his change, Tod; get him his change."

Tod retorted: "Get him his change! It's easy to say, sir; but look at the bill yourself."

The proprietor took a look, gave a low, eloquent whistle, then made a dive for the pile of rejected clothing, and began to snatch it this way and that, talking all the time excitedly, and as if to himself:

"Sell an **eccentric** millionaire such an unspeakable suit as that! Tod's a fool - a born fool. Always doing something like this. Drives every millionaire away from this place, because he can't tell a millionaire from a tramp, and never could. Ah, here's the thing I am after. Please get those things off, sir, and throw them in the fire. Do me the favor to put on this shirt and this suit; it's just the thing, the very thing - plain, rich, modest, and just ducally nobby; made to order for a foreign prince - you may know him, sir, his Serene Highness the Hospodar of Halifax; had to leave it with us and take a mourning-suit because his mother was going to die - which she didn't. But that's all right; we can't always have things the way we - that is, the way they - there!

---

perpetuated: maintained

eccentric: odd; unusual

trousers all right, they fit you to a charm, sir; now the waistcoat; aha, right again! now the coat - Lord! look at that, now! Perfect - the whole thing! I never saw such a triumph in all my experience."

I expressed my satisfaction.

"Quite right, sir, quite right; it'll do for a makeshift, I'm bound to say. But wait till you see what we'll get up for you on your own measure. Come, Tod, book and pen; get at it. Length of leg, 32" - and so on. Before I could get in a word he had measured me, and was giving orders for dress-suits, morning suits, shirts, and all sorts of things. When I got a chance I said:

"But, my dear sir, I *can't* give these orders, unless you can wait **indefinitely**, or change the bill."

"Indefinitely! It's a weak word, sir, a weak word. Eternally – *that's* the word, sir. Tod, rush these things through, and send them to the gentleman's address without any waste of time. Let the minor customers wait. Set down the gentleman's address and --"

"I'm changing my quarters. I will drop in and leave the new address."

"Quite right, sir, quite right. One moment - let me show you out, sir. There - good day, sir, good day."

Well, don't you see what was bound to happen? I drifted naturally into buying whatever I wanted, and asking for change. Within a week I was sumptuously equipped with all needful comforts and luxuries, and was housed in an expensive private

---

indefinitely: forever

hotel in Hanover Square. I took my dinners there, but for breakfast I stuck by Harris's humble feeding house, where I had got my first meal on my million-pound bill. I was the making of Harris. The fact had gone all abroad that the foreign crank who carried million-pound bills in his vest pocket was the patron saint of the place. That was enough. From being a poor, struggling, little hand-to-mouth enterprise, it had become celebrated, and overcrowded with customers. Harris was so grateful that he forced loans upon me, and would not be denied; and so, pauper as I was, I had money to spend, and was living like the rich and the great. I judged that there was going to be a crash by and by, but I was in, now, and must swim across or drown. You see there was just that element of **impending** disaster to give a serious side, a sober side, yes, a tragic side, to a state of things which would otherwise have been purely ridiculous. In the night, in the dark, the tragedy part was always to the front, and always warning, always threatening; and so I moaned and tossed, and sleep was hard to find. But in the cheerful daylight the tragedy element faded out and disappeared, and I walked on air, and was happy to giddiness, to intoxication, you may say.

And it was natural; for I had become one of the notorieties of the metropolis of the world, and it turned my head, not just a little, but a good deal. You could not take up a newspaper, English, Scotch, or Irish, without finding in it one or more references to the "vest-pocket million-pounder" and his latest doings and sayings. At first, in these mentions, I was at the

---

impending: approaching; about to occur soon

bottom of the personal-gossip column; next, I was listed above the knights, next above the baronets, next above the barons, and so on, and so on, climbing steadily, as my notoriety **augmented**, until I reached the highest altitude possible, and there I remained, taking precedence of all dukes not royal, and of all ecclesiastics except the primate of all England. But mind, this was not fame; as yet I had achieved only notoriety. Then came the climaxing stroke - the **accolade**, so to speak - which in a single instant transmuted the perishable dross of notoriety into the enduring gold of fame: *Punch* caricatured me! Yes, I was a made man now; my place was established. I might be joked about still, but **reverently**, not hilariously, not rudely; I could be smiled at, but not laughed at. The time for that had gone by. *Punch* pictured me all a-flutter with rags, dickering with a beef-eater for the Tower of London. Well, you can imagine how it was with a young fellow who had never been taken notice of before, and now all of a sudden couldn't say a thing that wasn't taken up and repeated everywhere; couldn't stir abroad without constantly overhearing the remark flying from lip to lip, "There he goes; that's him!" couldn't take his breakfast without a crowd to look on; couldn't appear in an opera-box without concentrating there the fire of a thousand lorgnettes. Why, I just swam in glory all day long - that is the amount of it.

You know, I even kept my old suit of rags, and every now

---

augmented: increased

accolade: award

reverently: respectfully

and then appeared in them, so as to have the old pleasure of buying trifles, and being insulted, and then shooting the scoffer dead with the million-pound bill. But I couldn't keep that up. The illustrated papers made the outfit so familiar that when I went out in it I was at once recognized and followed by a crowd, and if I attempted a purchase the man would offer me his whole shop on credit before I could pull my note on him.

About the tenth day of my fame I went to fulfill my duty to my flag by paying my respects to the American minister. He received me with the enthusiasm proper in my case, **upbraided** me for being so tardy in my duty, and said that there was only one way to get his forgiveness, and that was to take the seat at his dinner-party that night made vacant by the illness of one of his guests. I said I would, and we got to talking. It turned out that he and my father had been schoolmates in boyhood, Yale students together later, and always warm friends up to my father's death. So then he required me to put in at his house all the odd time I might have to spare, and I was very willing, of course.

In fact, I was more than willing; I was glad. When the crash should come, he might somehow be able to save me from total destruction; I didn't know how, but he might think of a way, maybe. I couldn't venture to unbosom myself to him at this late date, a thing which I would have been quick to do in the beginning of this awful career of mine in London. No, I couldn't venture it now; I was in too deep; that is, too deep for me to be

---

upbraided: scolded

risking **revelations** to so new a friend, though not clear beyond my depth, as *I* looked at it. Because, you see, with all my borrowing, I was carefully keeping within my means - I mean within my salary. Of course, I couldn't *know* what my salary was going to be, but I had a good enough basis for an estimate in the fact that if I won the bet I was to have *choice* of any situation in that rich old gentleman's gift provided I was competent - and I should certainly prove competent; I hadn't any doubt about that. And as to the bet, I wasn't worrying about that; I had always been lucky. Now my estimate of the salary was six hundred to a thousand a year; say, six hundred for the first year, and so on up year by year, till I struck the upper figure by proved merit. At present I was only in debt for my first year's salary. Everybody had been trying to lend me money, but I had fought off the most of them on one pretext or another; so this indebtedness represented only £300 borrowed money, the other £300 represented my keep and my purchases. I believed my second year's salary would carry me through the rest of the month if I went on being cautious and economical, and I intended to look sharply out for that. My month ended, my employer back from his journey, I should be all right once more, for I should at once divide the two years' salary among my creditors by assignment, and get right down to my work.

It was a lovely dinner-party of fourteen. The Duke and Duchess of Shoreditch, and their daughter the Lady Anne-Grace-Eleanor-Celeste-and-so-forth-and-so-forth-de-Bohun, the Earl

---

revelations: making known things that are surprising or secret

and Countess of Newgate, Viscount Cheapside, Lord and Lady Blatherskite, some untitled people of both sexes, the minister and his wife and daughter, and his daughter's visiting friend, an English girl of twenty-two, named Portia Langham, whom I fell in love with in two minutes, and she with me - I could see it without glasses. There was still another guest, an American - but I am a little ahead of my story. While the people were still in the drawing-room, whetting up for dinner, and coldly inspecting the late comers, the servant announced:

"Mr. Lloyd Hastings."

The moment the usual civilities were over, Hastings caught sight of me, and came straight with cordially outstretched hand; then stopped short when about to shake, and said, with an embarrassed look:

"I beg your pardon, sir, I thought I knew you."

"Why, you do know me, old fellow."

"No. Are *you* the - the--"

"Vest-pocket monster? I am, indeed. Don't be afraid to call me by my nickname; I'm used to it."

"Well, well, well, this is a surprise. Once or twice I've seen your own name coupled with the nickname, but it never occurred to me that *you* could be the Henry Adams referred to. Why, it isn't six months since you were clerking away for Blake Hopkins in Frisco on a salary, and sitting up nights on an extra allowance, helping me arrange and verify the Gould and Curry Extension papers and statistics. The idea of your being in London, and a vast millionaire, and a colossal celebrity! Why, it's the Arabian Nights come again. Man, I can't take it in at all; can't realize it;

give me time to settle the whirl in my head."

"The fact is, Lloyd, you are no worse off than I am. I can't realize it myself."

"Dear me, it *is* stunning, now isn't it? Why, it's just three months today since we went to the Miners' restaurant--"

"No; the What Cheer."

"Right, it *was* the What Cheer; went there at two in the morning, and had a chop and coffee after a hard six-hours grind over those Extension papers, and I tried to persuade you to come to London with me, and offered to get leave of absence for you and pay all your expenses, and give you something over if I succeeded in making the sale; and you would not listen to me, said I wouldn't succeed, and you couldn't afford to lose the run of business and be no end of time getting the hang of things again when you got back home. And yet here you are. How odd it all is! How did you happen to come, and whatever *did* give you this incredible start?"

"Oh, just an accident. It's a long story - a romance, a body may say. I'll tell you all about it, but not now."

"When?"

"The end of this month."

"That's more than a fortnight yet. It's too much of a strain on a person's curiosity. Make it a week."

"I can't. You'll know why, by and by. But how's the trade getting along?"

His cheerfulness vanished like a breath, and he said with a sigh:

"You were a true prophet, Hal, a true prophet. I wish I hadn't come. I don't want to talk about it."

"But you must. You must come and stop with me to-night, when we leave here, and tell me all about it."

"Oh, may I? Are you in earnest?" and the water showed in his eyes.

"Yes; I want to hear the whole story, every word."

"I'm so grateful! Just to find a human interest once more, in some voice and in some eye, in me and affairs of mine, after what I've been through here - lord! I could go down on my knees for it!"

He gripped my hand hard, and braced up, and was all right and lively after that for the dinner - which didn't come off. No; the usual thing happened, the thing that is always happening under that vicious and **aggravating** English system - the matter of precedence couldn't be settled, and so there was no dinner. Englishmen always eat dinner before they go out to dinner, because *they* know the risks they are running; but nobody ever warns the stranger, and so he walks placidly into the trap. Of course, nobody was hurt this time, because we had all been to dinner, none of us being novices excepting Hastings, and he having been informed by the minister at the time that he invited him that in deference to the English custom he had not provided any dinner. Everybody took a lady and processioned down to the dining-room because it is usual to go through the motions; but there the dispute began. The Duke of Shoreditch wanted to take precedence, and sit at the head of the table, holding that he

---

aggravating: annoying

placidly: in a calm way

outranked a minister who represented merely a nation and not a monarch; but I stood for my rights, and refused to yield. In the gossip column I ranked all dukes not royal, and said so, and claimed precedence of this one. It couldn't be settled, of course, struggle as we might and did, he finally (and **injudiciously**) trying to play birth and antiquity, and I "seeing" his Conqueror and "raising" him with Adam, whose direct **posterity** I was, as shown by my name, while *he* was of a **collateral** branch, as shown by *his*, and by his recent Norman origin; so we all processioned back to the drawing-room again and had a perpendicular lunch - plate of sardines and a strawberry, and you group yourself and stand up and eat it. Here the religion of precedence is not so **strenuous**; the two persons of highest rank chuck up a shilling, the one that wins has first go at his strawberry, and the loser gets the shilling. The next two chuck up, then the next two, and so on. After refreshment, tables were brought, and we all played cribbage, sixpence a game. The English never play any game for amusement. If they can't make something or lose something - they don't care which - they won't play.

We had a lovely time; certainly two of us had, Miss Langham and I. I was so bewitched with her that I couldn't count my hands if they went above a double sequence; and when I

---

injudiciously: thoughtlessly; tactlessly

posterity: descendant

collateral: of the same ancestry but a different branch

strenuous: requiring a lot of effort or energy

struck home I never discovered it, and started up the outside row again, and would have lost the game every time, only the girl did the same, she being in just my condition, you see; and consequently neither of us ever got out, or cared to wonder why we didn't; we only just knew we were happy, and didn't wish to know anything else, and didn't want to be interrupted. And I *told* her - I did, indeed - told her I loved her; and she - well, she blushed till her hair turned red, but she liked it; she *said* she did. Oh, there was never such an evening! Every time I pegged I put on a postscript; every time she pegged she acknowledged receipt of it, counting the hands the same. Why, I couldn't even say "Two for his heels" without adding "*My*, how sweet you do look!" and she would say, "Fifteen two, fifteen four, fifteen six, and a pair are eight, and eight are sixteen - *do* you think so?" - peeping out aslant from under her lashes, you know, so sweet and cunning. Oh, it was just *too*-too!

Well, I was perfectly honest and square with her; told her I hadn't a cent in the world but just the million-pound note she'd heard so much talk about, and *it* didn't belong to me, and that started her curiosity; and then I talked low, and told her the whole history right from the start, and it nearly killed her laughing. What in the nation she could find to laugh about *I* couldn't see, but there it was; every half-minute some new detail would fetch her, and I would have to stop as much as a minute and a half to give her a chance to settle down again. Why, she laughed herself lame - she did, indeed; I never saw anything like it. I mean I never saw a painful story - a story of a person's troubles and worries and fears - produce just *that* kind of effect before. So I loved her all the more, seeing she could be so cheerful when there wasn't anything to be cheerful about; for I might soon need that kind of wife, you know, the way things looked. Of course, I told her we should have to wait a couple of years, till I could catch up on my salary; but she didn't mind that, only she hoped I would be as careful as possible in the matter of expenses, and not let them run the least risk of trenching on our third year's pay. Then she began to get a little worried, and wondered if we were making any mistake, and starting the salary on a higher figure for the first year than I would get. This was good sense, and it made me feel a little less confident than I had been feeling before; but it gave me a good business idea, and I brought it frankly out.

"Portia, dear, would you mind going with me that day, when I confront those old gentlemen?"

She shrank a little, but said:

"N-o; if my being with you would help hearten you. But - would it be quite proper, do you think?"

"No, I don't know that it would - in fact, I'm afraid it wouldn't; but, you see, there's so *much* dependent upon it that--"

"Then I'll go anyway, proper or improper," she said, with a beautiful and generous enthusiasm. "Oh, I shall be so happy to think I'm helping!"

"Helping, dear? Why, you'll be doing it all. You're so beautiful and so lovely and so winning, that with you there I can pile our salary up till I break those good old fellows, and they'll never have the heart to struggle."

Sho! you should have seen the rich blood mount, and her

happy eyes shine!

"You wicked flatterer! There isn't a word of truth in what you say, but still I'll go with you. Maybe it will teach you not to expect other people to look with your eyes."

Were my doubts **dissipated**? Was my confidence restored? You may judge by this fact: privately I raised my salary to twelve hundred the first year on the spot. But I didn't tell her; I saved it for a surprise.

All the way home I was in the clouds, Hastings talking, I not hearing a word. When he and I entered my parlor, he brought me to myself with his fervent appreciations of my manifold comforts and luxuries.

"Let me just stand here a little and look my fill. Dear me! it's a palace - it's just a palace! And in it everything a body *could* desire, including cozy coal fire and supper standing ready. Henry, it doesn't merely make me realize how rich you are; it makes me realize, to the bone, to the marrow, how poor I am - how poor I am, and how miserable, how defeated, routed, **annihilated**!"

Plague take it! this language gave me the cold shudders. It scared me broad awake, and made me **comprehend** that I was standing on a half-inch crust, with a crater underneath. *I* didn't know I had been dreaming - that is, I hadn't been allowing myself to know it for a while back; but *now* - oh, dear! Deep in debt, not a cent in the world, a lovely girl's happiness or woe in

---

dissipated: disappeared
annihilated: destroyed
comprehend: understand

fervent: having a passionate intensity

my hands, and nothing in front of me but a salary which might never - oh, *would* never – **materialize**! Oh, oh, oh! I am ruined past hope! nothing can save me!

"Henry the mere unconsidered drippings of your daily income would --"

"Oh, my daily income! Here, down with this hot Scotch, and cheer up your soul. Here's with you! Or, no - you're hungry; sit down and --"

"Not a bite for me; I'm past it. I can't eat, these days; but I'll drink with you till I drop. Come!"

"Barrel for barrel, I'm with you! Ready? Here we go! Now, then, Lloyd, unreel your story while I brew."

"Unreel it? What, again?"

"Again? What do you mean by that?"

"Why, I mean do you want to hear it *over* again?"

"Do I want to hear it *over* again? This *is* a puzzler. Wait; don't take any more of that liquid. You don't need it."

"Look here, Henry, you alarm me. Didn't I tell you the whole story on the way here?"

"You?"

"Yes, I."

"I'll be hanged if I heard a word of it."

"Henry, this is a serious thing. It troubles me. What did you take up yonder at the minister's?"

Then it all flashed on me, and I owned up like a man.

"I took the dearest girl in this world - prisoner!"

---

materialize: be realized; happen

So then he came with a rush, and we shook, and shook, and shook till our hands ached; and he didn't blame me for not having heard a word of a story which had lasted while we walked three miles. He just sat down then, like the patient, good fellow he was, and told it all over again. Synopsized,* it amounted to this: He had come to England with what he thought was a grand opportunity; he had an "option" to sell the Gould and Curry Extension for the "locators" of it, and keep all he could get over a million dollars. He had worked hard, had pulled every wire he knew of, had left no honest expedient untried, had spent nearly all the money he had in the world, had not been able to get a solitary capitalist to listen to him, and his option would run out at the end of the month. In a word, he was ruined. Then he jumped up and cried out:

"Henry, you can save me! You can save me, and you're the only man in the universe that can. Will you do it? *Won't* you do it?"

"Tell me how. Speak out, my boy."

"Give me a million and my passage home for my 'option'! Don't, *don't* refuse!"

I was in a kind of agony. I was right on the point of coming out with the words, "Lloyd, I'm a pauper myself - absolutely penniless, and in *debt*!" But a white-hot idea came flaming through my head, and I gripped my jaws together, and calmed myself down till I was as cold as a capitalist. Then I said, in a commercial and self-possessed way:

"I will save you, Lloyd--"

"Then I'm already saved! God be merciful to you forever! If

synopsized: summarized

ever I --"

"Let me finish, Lloyd. I will save you, but not in that way; for that would not be fair to you, after your hard work, and the risks you've run. I don't need to buy mines; I can keep my capital moving, in a commercial center like London, without that; it's what I'm at, all the time; but here is what I'll do. I know all about that mine, of course; I know its immense value, and can swear to it if anybody wishes it. You shall sell out inside of the fortnight for three millions cash, using my name freely, and we'll divide, share and share alike."

Do you know, he would have danced the furniture to kindling-wood in his insane joy, and broken everything on the place, if I hadn't tripped him up and tied him.

Then he lay there, perfectly happy, saying:

"I may use your name! Your name - think of it! Man, they'll flock in droves, these rich Londoners; they'll *fight* for that stock! I'm a made man, I'm a made man forever, and I'll never forget you as long as I live!"

In less than twenty-four hours London was abuzz! I hadn't anything to do, day after day, but sit at home, and say to all comers:

"Yes; I told him to refer to me. I know the man, and I know the mine. His character is **above reproach**, and the mine is worth far more than he asks for it."

Meantime I spent all my evenings at the minister's with Portia. I didn't say a word to her about the mine; I saved it for a

---

above reproach: faultless; blameless

surprise. We talked salary; never anything but salary and love; sometimes love, sometimes salary, sometimes love and salary together. And my! the interest the minister's wife and daughter took in our little affair, and the endless ingenuities they invented to save us from interruption, and to keep the minister in the dark and unsuspicious - well, it was just lovely of them!

When the month was up at last, I had a million dollars to my credit in the London and County Bank, and Hastings was fixed in the same way. Dressed at my level best, I drove by the house in Portland Place, judged by the look of things that my birds were home again, went on toward the minister's and got my precious, and we started back, talking salary with all our might. She was so excited and anxious that it made her just intolerably beautiful. I said:

"Dearie, the way you're looking it's a crime to strike for a salary a single penny under three thousand a year."

"Henry, Henry, you'll ruin us!"

"Don't you be afraid. Just keep up those looks, and trust to me. It'll all come out right."

So, as it turned out, I had to keep **bolstering** up *her* courage all the way. She kept pleading with me, and saying:

"Oh, please remember that if we ask too much we may get no salary at all; and then what will become of us, with no way in the world to earn our living?"

We were ushered in by that same servant, and there they were, the two old gentlemen. Of course, they were surprised to

---

bolstering: boosting; strengthening

see that wonderful creature with me, but I said:

"It's all right, gentlemen; she is my future stay and helpmate."

And I introduced them to her, and called them by name. It didn't surprise them; they knew I would know enough to consult the directory. They seated us, and were very polite to me, and very **solicitous** to relieve her from embarrassment, and put her as much at her ease as they could. Then I said:

"Gentlemen, I am ready to report."

"We are glad to hear it," said *my* man, "for now we can decide the bet which my brother Abel and I made. If you have won for me, you shall have any situation in my gift. Have you the million-pound note?"

"Here it is, sir," and I handed it to him.

"I've won!" he shouted, and slapped Abel on the back. "Now what do you say, brother?"

"I say he *did* survive, and I've lost twenty thousand pounds. I never would have believed it."

"I've a further report to make," I said, "and a pretty long one. I want you to let me come soon, and detail my whole month's history; and I promise you it's worth hearing. Meantime, take a look at that."

"What, man! Certificate of deposit for £200,000. Is it yours?"

"Mine. I earned it by thirty days' **judicious** use of that little

---

solicitous: careful; anxious

judicious: wise: sensible

loan you let me have. And the only use I made of it was to buy trifles and offer the bill in change."

"Come, this is astonishing! It's incredible, man!"

"Never mind, I'll prove it. Don't take my word unsupported."

But now Portia's turn was come to be surprised. Her eyes were spread wide, and she said:

"Henry, is that really your money? Have you been fibbing to me?"

"I have, indeed, dearie. But you'll forgive me, I know."

She put up an arch pout, and said:

"Don't you be so sure. You are a naughty thing to deceive me so!"

"Oh, you'll get over it, sweetheart, you'll get over it; it was only fun, you know. Come, let's be going."

"But wait, wait! The situation, you know. I want to give you the situation," said my man.

"Well," I said, "I'm just as grateful as I can be, but really I don't want one."

"But you can have the very choicest one in my gift."

"Thanks again, with all my heart; but I don't even want *that* one."

"Henry, I'm ashamed of you. You don't half thank the good gentleman. May I do it for you?"

"Indeed, you shall, dear, if you can improve it. Let us see you try."

She walked to my man, got up in his lap, put her arm round his neck, and kissed him right on the mouth. Then the two old gentlemen shouted with laughter, but I was dumbfounded, just petrified, as you may say. Portia said:

"Papa, he has said you haven't a situation in your gift that he'd take; and I feel just as hurt as --"

"My darling, is that your papa?"

"Yes; he's my step-papa, and the dearest one that ever was. You understand now, don't you, why I was able to laugh when you told me at the minister's, not knowing my relationships, what trouble and worry papa's and Uncle Abel's scheme was giving you?"

Of course, I spoke right up now, without any fooling, and went straight to the point.

"Oh, my dearest dear sir, I want to take back what I said. You *have* got a situation open that I want."

"Name it."

"Son-in-law."

"Well, well, well! But you know, if you haven't ever served in that capacity, you, of course, can't furnish recommendations of a sort to satisfy the conditions of the contract, and so--"

"Try me - oh, do, I beg of you! Only just try me thirty or forty years, and if --"

"Oh, well, all right; it's but a little thing to ask, take her along."

Happy, we two? There are not words enough in the unabridged to describe it. And when London got the whole history, a day or two later, of my month's adventures with that bank-note, and how they ended, did London talk, and have a good time? Yes.

My Portia's papa took that friendly and hospitable bill back to the Bank of England and cashed it; then the Bank canceled it and made him a present of it, and he gave it to us at our wedding, and it has always hung in its frame in the sacredest place in our home ever since. For it gave me my Portia. But for it I could not have remained in London, would not have appeared at the minister's, never should have met her. And so I always say, "Yes, it's a million-pounder, as you see; but it never made but one purchase in its life, and *then* got the article for only about a tenth part of its value."

Lord Arthur Savile's Crime

I

It was Lady Windermere's last reception before Easter, and Bentinck House was even more crowded than usual. Six Cabinet Ministers had come on from the Speaker's Levée in their stars and ribands, all the pretty women wore their smartest dresses, and at the end of the picture-gallery stood the Princess Sophia of Carlsrühe, a heavy Tartar-looking lady, with tiny black eyes and wonderful emeralds, talking bad French at the top of her voice, and laughing **immoderately** at everything that was said to her. It was certainly a wonderful **medley** of people. Gorgeous peeresses chatted affably to violent Radicals, popular preachers brushed coat-tails with eminent sceptics, a perfect bevy of bishops kept following a stout prima-donna from room to room, on the staircase stood several Royal Academicians, disguised as artists, and it was said that at one time the supper-room was absolutely crammed with geniuses. In fact, it was one of Lady Windermere's best nights, and the Princess stayed till nearly half-past eleven.

As soon as she had gone, Lady Windermere returned to the picture-gallery, where a celebrated political economist was

---

immoderately: too much

medley: variety

solemnly explaining the scientific theory of music to an **indignant virtuoso** from Hungary, and began to talk to the Duchess of Paisley. She looked wonderfully beautiful with her grand ivory throat, her large blue forget-me-not eyes, and her heavy coils of golden hair. *Or pur* they were – not that pale straw colour that nowadays **usurps** the gracious name of gold, but such gold as is woven into sunbeams or hidden in strange amber; and they gave to her face something of the fame of a saint, with not a little of the fascination of a sinner. She was a curious psychological study. Early in life she had discovered the important truth that nothing looks so like innocence as an **indiscretion**; and by a series of **reckless escapades**, half of them quite harmless, she had acquired all the privileges of a personality. She had more than once changed her husband; indeed, Debrett credits her with three marriages; but as she had never changed her lover, the world had long ago ceased to talk scandal about her. She was now forty years of age, childless, and with that **inordinate** passion for pleasure which is the secret of remaining young.

---

indignant: upset
virtuoso: expert musician
or pur: (French) pure gold
usurps: claims wrongfully
indiscretion: misconduct; social offence
reckless: irresponsible risk-taking
escapades: adventures
inordinate: extreme

Suddenly she looked eagerly round the room, and said, in her clear contralto voice, "Where is my chiromantist?"[1]

"Your what, Gladys?" exclaimed the Duchess, giving an involuntary start.

"My chiromantist, Duchess; I can't live without him at present."

"Dear Gladys! you are always so original," murmured the Duchess, trying to remember what a chiromantist really was, and hoping it was not the same as a chiropodist.[2]

"He comes to see my hand twice a week regularly," continued Lady Windermere, "and is most interesting about it."

"Good heavens!" said the Duchess to herself, "he is a sort of chiropodist after all. How very dreadful. I hope he is a foreigner at any rate. It wouldn't be quite so bad then."

"I must certainly introduce him to you."

"Introduce him!" cried the Duchess; "you don't mean to say he is here?" and she began looking about for a small tortoise-shell fan and a very tattered lace shawl, so as to be ready to go at a moment's notice.

"Of course he is here; I would not dream of giving a party without him. He tells me I have a pure psychic hand, and that if my thumb had been the least little bit shorter, I should have been a confirmed pessimist, and gone into a convent."

"Oh, I see!" said the Duchess, feeling very much relieved; "he tells fortunes, I suppose?"

"And misfortunes, too," answered Lady Windermere, "any amount of them. Next year, for instance, I am in great danger, both by land and sea, so I am going to live in a balloon, and draw

1 a person who uses hands to tell that person's fortune - Chiromanist

2 a person treats feet - chiropodist

up my dinner in a basket every evening. It is all written down on my little finger, or on the palm of my hand, I forget which."

"But surely that is tempting Providence, Gladys."

"My dear Duchess, surely Providence can resist temptation by this time. I think every one should have their hands told once a month so as to know what not to do. Of course, one does it all the same, but it is so pleasant to be warned. Now if some one doesn't go and fetch Mr. Podgers at once, I shall have to go myself."

"Let me go, Lady Windermere," said a tall handsome young man, who was standing by, listening to the conversation with an amused smile.

"Thanks so much, Lord Arthur; but I am afraid you wouldn't recognise him."

"If he is as wonderful as you say, Lady Windermere, I couldn't well miss him. Tell me what he is like, and I'll bring him to you at once."

"Well, he is not a bit like a chiromantist. I mean he is not mysterious, or **esoteric**, or romantic-looking. He is a little, stout man, with a funny, bald head, and great gold-rimmed spectacles; something between a family doctor and a country attorney. I'm really very sorry, but it is not my fault. People are so annoying. All my pianists look exactly like poets, and all my poets look exactly like pianists; and I remember last season asking a most dreadful **conspirator** to dinner, a man who had blown up ever so

---

esoteric: difficult to understand

conspirator: plotter of secret plans especially for wrongdoing

many people, and always wore a coat of mail, and carried a dagger up his shirt-sleeve; and do you know that when he came he looked just like a nice old clergyman, and cracked jokes all the evening? Of course, he was very amusing, and all that, but I was awfully disappointed; and when I asked him about the coat of mail, he only laughed, and said it was far too cold to wear in England. Ah, here is Mr. Podgers! Now, Mr. Podgers, I want you to tell the Duchess of Paisley's hand. Duchess, you must take your glove off. No, not the left hand, the other."

"Dear Gladys, I really don't think it is quite right," said the Duchess, feebly unbuttoning a rather soiled kid glove.

"Nothing interesting ever is," said Lady Windermere: "*on a fait le monde ainsi*. But I must introduce you. Duchess, this is Mr. Podgers, my pet chiromantist. Mr. Podgers, this is the Duchess of Paisley, and if you say that she has a larger mountain of the moon than I have, I will never believe in you again."

"I am sure, Gladys, there is nothing of the kind in my hand," said the Duchess gravely.

"Your Grace is quite right," said Mr. Podgers, glancing at the little fat hand with its short square fingers, "the mountain of the moon is not developed. The line of life, however, is excellent. Kindly bend the wrist. Thank you. Three distinct lines on the *rascette*! You will live to a great age, Duchess, and be extremely happy. Ambition - very moderate, line of intellect not exaggerated, line of heart -"

---

on a fait le monde ainsi: (French) the world is built this way

rascette: part of the wrist below the palm

"Now, do be indiscreet, Mr. Podgers," cried Lady Windermere.

"Nothing would give me greater pleasure," said Mr. Podgers, bowing, "if the Duchess ever had been, but I am sorry to say that I see great permanence[1] of affection, combined with a strong sense of duty."

"Pray go on, Mr. Podgers," said the Duchess, looking quite pleased.

"Economy is not the least of your Grace's virtues," continued Mr. Podgers, and Lady Windermere went off into fits of laughter.

"Economy is a very good thing," remarked the Duchess **complacently**; "when I married Paisley he had eleven castles, and not a single house fit to live in."

"And now he has twelve houses, and not a single castle," cried Lady Windermere.

"Well, my dear," said the Duchess, "I like –"

"Comfort," said Mr. Podgers, "and modern improvements, and hot water laid on in every bedroom. Your Grace is quite right. Comfort is the only thing our civilisation can give us."

"You have told the Duchess's character admirably, Mr. Podgers, and now you must tell Lady Flora's"; and in answer to a nod from the smiling hostess, a tall girl, with sandy Scotch hair, and high shoulder-blades, stepped awkwardly from behind the sofa, and held out a long, bony hand with spatulate[2] fingers.

"Ah, a pianist! I see," said Mr. Podgers, "an excellent pianist, but perhaps hardly a musician. Very reserved, very honest, and

---

complacently: in a self-satisfied way

1 remaining unchanged forever - permanence

2 having a rounded end - spatulate

with a great love of animals."

"Quite true!" exclaimed the Duchess, turning to Lady Windermere, "absolutely true! Flora keeps two dozen collie dogs at Macloskie, and would turn our town house into a **menagerie** if her father would let her."

"Well, that is just what I do with my house every Thursday evening," cried Lady Windermere, laughing, "only I like lions better than collie dogs."

"Your one mistake, Lady Windermere," said Mr. Podgers, with a pompous bow.

"If a woman can't make her mistakes charming, she is only a female," was the answer. "But you must read some more hands for us. Come, Sir Thomas, show Mr. Podgers yours"; and a genial-looking old gentleman, in a white waistcoat, came forward, and held out a thick rugged hand, with a very long third finger.

"An adventurous nature; four long voyages in the past, and one to come. Been shipwrecked three times. No, only twice, but in danger of a shipwreck your next journey. A strong Conservative, very punctual, and with a passion for collecting curiosities. Had a severe illness between the ages of sixteen and eighteen. Was left a fortune when about thirty. Great **aversion** to cats and Radicals."

"Extraordinary!" exclaimed Sir Thomas; "you must really tell my wife's hand, too."

---

menagerie: zoo

aversion: strong dislike

"Your second wife's," said Mr. Podgers quietly, still keeping Sir Thomas's hand in his. "Your second wife's. I shall be charmed"; but Lady Marvel, a melancholy-looking woman, with brown hair and sentimental eyelashes, entirely declined to have her past or her future exposed; and nothing that Lady Windermere could do would induce Monsieur de Koloff, the Russian Ambassador, even to take his gloves off. In fact, many people seemed afraid to face the odd little man with his stereotyped smile, his gold spectacles, and his bright, beady eyes; and when he told poor Lady Fermor right out before every one, that she did not care a bit for music, but was extremely fond of musicians, it was generally felt that chiromancy was a most dangerous science, and one that ought not to be encouraged, except in a **tête-à-tête**.

Lord Arthur Savile, however, who did not know anything about Lady Fermor's unfortunate story, and who had been watching Mr. Podgers with a great deal of interest, was filled with an immense curiosity to have his own hand read, and feeling somewhat shy about putting himself forward, crossed over the room to where Lady Windermere was sitting, and, with a charming blush, asked her if she thought Mr. Podgers would mind.

"Of course, he won't mind," said Lady Windermere, "that is what he is here for. All my lions, Lord Arthur, are performing lions, and jump through hoops whenever I ask them. But I must warn you beforehand that I shall tell Sybil everything. She is

---

tête-à-tête: private talk between two people

coming to lunch with me to-morrow, to talk about bonnets, and if Mr. Podgers finds out that you have a bad temper, or a tendency to gout, or a wife living in Bayswater, I shall certainly let her know all about it."

Lord Arthur smiled, and shook his head. "I am not afraid," he answered. "Sybil knows me as well as I know her."

"Ah! I am a little sorry to hear you say that. The proper basis for marriage is a mutual misunderstanding. No, I am not at all **cynical**, I have merely got experience, which, however, is very much the same thing. Mr. Podgers, Lord Arthur Savile is dying to have his hand read. Don't tell him that he is engaged to one of the most beautiful girls in London, because that appeared in the *Morning Post* a month ago."

"Dear Lady Windermere," cried the Marchioness of Jedburgh, "do let Mr. Podgers stay here a little longer. He has just told me I should go on the stage, and I am so interested."

"If he has told you that, Lady Jedburg, I shall certainly take him away. Come over at once, Mr. Podgers, and read Lord Arthur's hand."

"Well," said Lady Jedburgh, making a little *moue* as she rose from the sofa, "if I am not to be allowed to go on the stage, I must be allowed to be part of the audience at any rate."

"Of course; we are all going to be part of the audience," said Lady Windermere; "and now, Mr. Podgers, be sure and tell us

---

cynical: disbelieving in the sincerity or goodness of human actions

moue: grimace showing displeasure; pout

something nice. Lord Arthur is one of my special favourites."

But when Mr. Podgers saw Lord Arthur's hand he grew curiously pale, and said nothing. A shudder seemed to pass through him, and his great bushy eyebrows twitched **convulsively**, in an odd, irritating way they had when he was puzzled. Then some huge beads of perspiration broke out on his yellow forehead, like a poisonous dew, and his fat fingers grew cold and clammy.

Lord Arthur did not fail to notice these strange signs of agitation, and, for the first time in his life, he himself felt fear. His impulse was to rush from the room, but he restrained himself. It was better to know the worst, whatever it was, than to be left in this hideous uncertainty.

"I am waiting, Mr. Podgers," he said.

"We are all waiting," cried Lady Windermere, in her quick, impatient manner, but the chiromantist made no reply.

"I believe Arthur is going on the stage," said Lady Jedburgh, "and that, after your scolding, Mr. Podgers is afraid to tell him so."

Suddenly Mr. Podgers dropped Lord Arthur's right hand, and seized hold of his left, bending down so low to examine it that the gold rims of his spectacles seemed almost to touch the palm. For a moment his face became a white mask of horror, but he soon recovered his *sang-froid*, and looking up at Lady Windermere, said with a forced smile, "It is the hand of a

---

convulsively: involuntarily; like a spasm

sang-froid: calmness under strain

charming young man."

"Of course it is!" answered Lady Windermere, "but will he be a charming husband? That is what I want to know."

"All charming young men are," said Mr. Podgers.

"I don't think a husband should be too fascinating," murmured Lady Jedburgh **pensively**, "it is so dangerous."

"My dear child, they never are too fascinating," cried Lady Windermere. "But what I want are details. Details are the only things that interest. What is going to hapeen to Lord Arthur?"

"Well, within the next few months Lord Arthur will go on a voyage -"

"Oh yes, his honeymmon, of course!"

"And lose a relative."

"Not his sister, I hope?" said Lady Jedburgh, in a piteous tone of voice.

"Certainly not his sister," answered Mr. Podgers, with a deprecating wave of the hand, "a distant relative merely."

"Well, I am dreadfully disappointed," said Lady Windermere. "I have absolutely nothing to tell Sybil to-morrow. No one cares about distant relatives nowadays. They went out of fashion years ago. However, I suppose she had better have a black silk by her; it always does for church, you know. And now let us go to supper. They are sure to have eaten everything up, but we may find some hot soup. François used to make excellent soup once, but he is so agitated about politics at present, that I never feel

---

pensively: thinking seriously

quite certain about him. I do wish General Boulanger would keep quiet. Duchess, I am sure you are tired?"

"Not at all, dear Gladys," answered the Duchess, waddling towards the door. "I have enjoyed myself immensely, and the chiropodist, I mean the chiromantist, is most interesting. Flora, where can my tortoise-shell fan be? Oh, thank you, Sir Thomas, so much. And my lace shawl, Flora? Oh, thank you, Sir Thomas, very kind, I'm sure"; and the worthy creature finally managed to get downstairs without dropping her scent-bottle more than twice.

All this time Lord Arthur Savile had remained standing by the fireplace, with the same feeling of dread over him, the same sickening sense of coming evil. He smiled sadly at his sister, as she swept past him on Lord Plymdale's arm, looking lovely in her pink brocade and pearls, and he hardly heard Lady Windermere when she called to him to follow her. He thought of Sybil Merton, and the idea that anything could come between them made his eyes dim with tears.

Looking at him, one would have said that Nemesis had stolen the shield of Pallas, and shown him the Gorgon's head. He seemed turned to stone, and his face was like marble in its melancholy. He had lived the delicate and luxurious life of a young man of birth and fortune, a life exquisite in its freedom from sordid care, its beautiful boyish **insouciance**; and now for the first time he became conscious of the terrible mystery of Destiny, of the awful meaning of Doom.

How mad and monstrous it all seemed! Could it be that

---

insouciance: carefreeness; unconcern

written on his hand, in characters that he could not read himself, but that another could decipher, was some fearful secret of sin, some blood-red sign of crime? Was there no escape possible? Were we no better than chessmen, moved by an unseen power, vessels the potter fashions at his fancy, for honour or for shame? His reason revolted against it, and yet he felt that some tragedy was hanging over him, and that he had been suddenly called upon to bear an intolerable burden. Actors are so fortunate. They can choose whether they will appear in tragedy or in comedy, whether they will suffer or make merry, laugh or shed tears. But in real life it is different. Most men and women are forced to perform parts for which they have no qualifications. Our Guildensterns play Hamlet for us, and our Hamlets have to jest like Prince Hal. The world is a stage, but the play is badly cast.

Suddenly Mr. Podgers entered the room. When he saw Lord Arthur he started, and his coarse, fat face became a sort of greenish-yellow colour. The two men's eyes met, and for a moment there was silence.

"The Duchess has left one of her gloves here, Lord Arthur, and has asked me to bring it to her," said Mr. Podgers finally. "Ah, I see it on the sofa! Good evening."

"Mr. Podgers, I must insist on your giving me a straightforward answer to a question I am going to put to you."

"Another time, Lord Arthur, but the Duchess is anxious. I am afraid I must go."

"You shall not go. The Duchess is in no hurry."

"Ladies should not be kept waiting, Lord Arthur," said Mr. Podgers, with his sickly smile. "The fair sex is apt to be impatient."

Lord Arthur's finely-chiselled lips curled in **petulant disdain**. The poor Duchess seemed to him of very little importance at that moment. He walked across the room to where Mr. Podgers was standing, and held his hand out.

"Tell me what you saw there," he said. "Tell me the truth. I must know it. I am not a child."

Mr. Podgers's eyes blinked behind his gold-rimmed spectacles, and he moved uneasily from one foot to the other, while his fingers played nervously with a flash watch-chain.

"What makes you think that I saw anything in your hand, Lord Arthur, more than I told you?"

"I know you did, and I insist on your telling me what it was. I will pay you. I will give you a cheque for a hundred pounds."

The green eyes flashed for a moment, and then became dull again.

"Guineas?" said Mr. Podgers at last, in a low voice.

"Certainly. I will send you a cheque to-morrow. What is your club?"

"I have no club. That is to say, not just at present. My address is - , but allow me to give you my card"; and producing a bit of gilt-edge pasteboard from his waistcoat pocket, Mr. Podgers handed it, with a low bow, to Lord Arthur, who read on it, "*Mr. Septimus R. Podgers, Professional Chiromantist, 1030 West Moon Street.*"

---

petulant: annoyed

disdain: contempt; scorn

"My hours are from ten to four," murmured Mr. Podgers mechanically, "and I make a reduction for families."

"Be quick," cried Lord Arthur, looking very pale, and holding his hand out.

Mr. Podgers glanced nervously round, and drew the heavy *portière* across the door.

"It will take a little time, Lord Arthur, you had better sit down."

"Be quick, sir," cried Lord Arthur again, stamping his foot angrily on the polished floor.

Mr. Podgers smiled, drew from his breast-pocket a small magnifying glass, and wiped it carefully with his handkerchief.

"I am quite ready," he said.

II

Ten minutes later, with face blanched by terror, and eyes wild with grief, Lord Arthur Savile rushed from Bentinck House, crushing his way through the crowd of fur-coated footmen that stood round the large striped awning, and seeming not to see or hear anything. The night was bitter cold, and the gas-lamps round the square flared and flickered in the keen wind; but his hands were hot with fever, and his forehead burned like fire. On and on he went, almost with the **gait** of a drunken man. A

---

portière: (French) door-curtain

gait: manner of walking

policeman looked curiously at him as he passed, and a beggar, who slouched from an archway to ask for alms, grew frightened, seeing misery greater than his own. Once he stopped under a lamp, and looked at his hands. He thought he could detect the stain of blood already upon them, and a faint cry broke from his trembling lips.

Murder! that is what the chiromantist had seen there. Murder! The vey night seemed to know it, and the desolate wind to howl it in his ear. The dark corners of the streets were full of it. It grinned at him from the roofs of the houses.

First he came to the Park, whose sombre woodland seemed to fascinate him. He leaned wearily up against the raililings, cooling his brow against the wet metal, and listening to the tremulous silence of the trees. "Murder! murder!" he kept repeating, as though **iteration** could dim the horror of the word. The sound of his own voice made him shudder, yet he almost hoped that Echo might hear him, and wake the slumbering city from its dreams. He felt a mad desire to stop the casual passer-by, and tell him everything.

Then he wandered across Oxford Street into narrow, shameful alleys. Two women with painted faces mocked at him as he went by. From a dark courtyard came a sound of oaths and blows, followed by shrill screams, and, huddled upon a damp door-step, he saw the crooked-back forms of poverty and eld. A strange pity came over him. Were these children of sin and misery predestined to their end, as he to his? Were they, like him,

---

iteration: repetition

vey: used to express dismay

merely the puppets of a monstrous show?

And yet it was not the mystery, but the comedy of suffering that struck him; its absolute uselessness, its grotesque want of meaning. How incoherent everything seemed! How lacking in all harmony! He was amazed at the **discord** between the shallow optimism of the day, and the real facts of existence. He was still very young.

After a time he found himself in front of Marylebone Church. The silent roadway looked like a long riband of polished silver, flecked here and there by the dark arabesques of waving shadows. Far into the distance curved the line of flickering gas-lamps, and outside a little walled-in house stood a solitary hansom, the driver asleep inside. He walked hastily in the direction of Portland Place, now and then looking round, as though he feared that he was being followed. At the corner of Rich Street stood two men, reading a small bill upon a hoarding. An odd feeling of curiosity stirred him, and he crossed over. As he came near, the word "Murder," printed in black letters, met his eye. He started, and a deep flush came into his cheek. It was an advertisement offering a reward for any information leading to the arrest of a man of medium height, between thirty and forty years of age, wearing a billycock hat, a black coat, and check trousers, and with a scar upon his right cheek. He read it over and over again, and wondered if the wretched man would be caught, and how he had been scarred. Perhaps, some day, his own name might be placarded on the walls of London. Some day,

---

discord: difference; disharmony; conflict

perhaps, a price would be set on his head also.

The thought made him sick with horror. He turned on his heel, and hurried on into the night.

Where he went he hardly knew. He had a dim memory of wandering through a labyrinth of sordid houses, of being lost in a giant web of sombre streets, and it was bright dawn when he found himself at last in Piccadilly Circus. As he strolled home towards Belgrave Square, he met the great waggons on their way to Covent Garden. The white-smocked carters, with their pleasant sunburnt faces and coarse curly hair, strode sturdily on, cracking their whips, and calling out now and then to each other; on the back of a huge grey horse, the leader of a jangling team, sat a chubby boy, with a bunch of primroses in his battered hat, keeping tight hold of the mane with his little hands, and laughing; and the great piles of vegetables looked like masses of jade against the morning sky, like masses of green jade against the pink petals of some marvellous rose. Lord Arthur felt curiously affected, he could not tell why. There was something in the dawn's delicate loveliness that seemed to him inexpressibly pathetic, and he thought of all the days that break in beauty, and that set in storm. These rustics, too, with their rough, good-humoured voices, and their **nonchalant** ways, what a strange London they saw! A London free from the sin of night and the smoke of day, a pallid, ghost-like city, a desolate town of tombs! He wondered what they thought of it, and whether they knew anything of its splendour and its shame, of its fierce, fiery-

---

nonchalant: indifferent

coloured joys, and its horrible hunger, of all it makes and mars from morn to eve. Probably it was to them merely a mart where they brought their fruit to sell, and where they tarried for a few hours at most, leaving the streets still silent, the houses still asleep. It gave him pleasure to watch them as they went by. Rude as they were, with their heavy, hob-nailed shoes, and their awkward gait, they brought a little of Arcady with them. He felt that they had lived with Nature, and that she had taught them peace. He envied them all that they did not know.

By the time he had reached Belgrave Square the sky was a faint blue, and the birds were beginning to twitter in the gardens.

III

When Lord Arthur woke it was twelve o'clock, and the midday sun was streaming through the ivory-silk curtains of his room. He got up and looked out of the window. A dim haze of heat was hanging over the great city, and the roofs of the houses were like dull silver. In the flickering green of the square below some children were flitting about like white butterflies, and the pavement was crowded with people on their way to the Park. Never had life seemed lovelier to him, never had the things of evil seemed more remote.

Then his valet brought him a cup of chocolate on a tray. After he had drunk it, he drew aside a heavy *portière* of peach-coloured plush, and passed into the bathroom. The light stole softly from above, through thin slabs of transparent onyx, and

onyx: a semiprecious variety of agate with different colors in layers

the water in the marble tank glimmered like a moonstone. He plunged hastily in, till the cool ripples touched throat and hair, and then dipped his head right under, as though he would have wiped away the stain of some shameful memory. When he stepped out he felt almost at peace. The exquisitive physical conditions of the moment had dominated him, as indeed often happens in the case of very finely-wrought natures, for the senses, like fire, can purify as well as destroy.

After breakfast, he flung himself down on a divan and lit a cigarette. On the mantel-shelf, framed in dainty old brocade, stood a large photograph of Sybil Merton, as he had seen her first at Lady Noel's ball. The small, exquisitively-shaped head drooped slightly to one side, as though the thin, reed-like throat could hardly bear the burden of so much beauty; the lips were slightly parted, and seemed made for sweet music; and all the tender purity of girlhood looked out in wonder from the dreaming eyes. With her soft, clinging dress of *crêpe-de-chine*, and her large leaf-shaped fan, she looked like one of those delicate little figures men find in the olive-woods near Tanagra; and there was a touch of Greek grace in her pose and attitude. Yet she was not *petite*. She was simply perfectly proportioned - a rare thing in an age when so many women are either over life-size or insignificant.

Now as Lord Arthur looked at her, he was filled with the terrible pity that is born of love. He felt that to marry her, with the doom of murder hanging over his head, would be a betrayal

---

crêpe-de-chine: thin crinkled fabric

like that of Judas, a sin worse than any the Borgia had ever dreamed of. What happiness could there be for them, when at any moment he might be called upon to carry out the awful prophecy written in his hand? What manner of life would be theirs while Fate still held this fearful fortune in the scales? The marriage must be postponed, at all costs. Of this he was quite **resolved**. Ardently though he loved the girl, and the mere touch of her fingers, when they sat together, made each nerve of his body thrill with exquisitive joy, he recognised none the less clearly where his duty lay, and was fully conscious of the fact that he had no right to marry until he had committed the murder. This done, he could stand before the altar with Sybil Merton, and give his life into her hands without terror of wrongdoing. This done, he could take her to his arms, knowing that she would never have to blush for him, never have to hang her head in shame. But done it must be first; and the sooner the better for both.

Many men in his position would have preferred the primrose path of dalliance to the steep heights of duty; but Lord Arthur was too **conscientious** to set pleasure above principle. There was more than mere passion in his love; and Sybil was to him a symbol of all that is good and noble. For a moment he had a natural **repugnance** against what he was asked to do, but it soon

---

resolved: determined

conscientious: careful to do the right thing to the best of one's ability

repugnance: disgust; strong dislike

passed away. His heart told him that it was not a sin, but a sacrifice; his reason reminded him that there was no other course open. He had to choose between living for himself and living for others, and terrible though the task laid upon him undoubtedly was, yet he knew that he must not suffer selfishness to triumph over love. Sooner or later we are all called upon to decide on the same issue - of us all, the same question is asked. To Lord Arthur it came early in life - before his nature had been spoiled by the calculating cynicism of middle-age, or his heart corroded by the shallow, fashionable egotism of our day, and he felt no hesitation about doing his duty. Fortunately also, for him, he was no mere dreamer, or idle dilettante.* Had he been so, he would have hesitated, like Hamlet, and let irresolution mar his purpose. But he was essentially practical. Life to him meant action, rather than thought. He had that rarest of all things, common sense.

The wild, **turbid** feelings of the previous night had by this time completely passed away, and it was almost with a sense of shame that he looked back upon his mad wanderings from street to street, his fierce emotional agony. The very sincerity of his sufferings made them seem unreal to him now. He wondered how he could have been so foolish as to rant and rave about the inevitable. The only question that seemed to trouble him was, whom to make away with; for he was not blind to the fact that murder, like the religions of the Pagan world, requires a victim as well as a priest. Not being a genius, he had no enemies, and indeed he felt that this was not the time for the gratification of

---

turbid: very confused

*a person who grows an interest without commintment or knowlegde

any personal pique or dislike, the mission in which he was engaged being one of great and grave solemnity*. He accordingly made out a list of his friends and relatives on a sheet of notepaper, and after careful consideration, decided in favour of Lady Clementina Beauchamp, a dear old lady who lived in Curzon Street, and was his own second cousin by his mother's side. He had always been very fond of Lady Clem, as every one called her, and as he was very wealthy himself, having come into all Lord Rugby's property when he came of age, there was no possibility of his deriving any vulgar monetary advantage by her death. In fact, the more he thought over the matter, the more she seemed to him to be just the right person, and, feeling that any delay would be unfair to Sybil, he determined to make his arrangements at once.

The first thing to be done was, of course, to settle with the chiromantist; so he sat down at a small Sheraton writing-table that stood near the window, drew a cheque for £105, payable to the oder of Mr. Septimus Podgers, and, enclosing it in an envelope, told his valet to take it to West Moon Street. He then telephoned to the stables for his hansom, and dressed to go out. As he was leaving the room he looked back at Sybil Merton's photograph, and swore that, come what may, he would never let her know what he was doing for her sake, but would keep the secret of his self-sacrifice hidden always in his heart.

On his way to the Buckingham, he stopped at a florist's, and sent Sybil a beautiful basket of narcissi, with lovely white petals and staring pheasants' eyes, and on arriving at the club went straight to the library, rang the bell, and ordered the waiter to

* the state of being serious

bring him a lemon-and-soda, and a book on Toxicology. He had fully decided that poison was the best means to adopt in this troublesome business. Anything like personal violence was extremely distasteful to him, and besides, he was vey anxious not to muder Lady Clementina in any way that might attract public attention, as he hated the idea of being lionised at Lady Windermere's, or seeing his name figuring in the paragraphs of vulgar society- newspapers. He had also to think of Sybil's father and mother, who were rather old-fashioned people, and might possibly object to the marriage if there was anything like a scandal, though he felt certain that if he told them the whole facts of the case they would be the very first to appreciate the motives that had actuated him. He had every reason, then, to decide in favour of poison. It was safe, sure, and quiet, and did away with any necessity for painful scenes, to which, like most Englishmen, he had a rooted objection.

Of the science of poisons, however, he knew absolutely nothing, and as the waiter seemed quite unable to find anything in the library but *Ruff's Guide* and *Bailey's Magazine*, he examined the book-shelves himself, and finally came across a handsomely-bound edition of the *Pharmacopoeia*, and a copy of Erskine's *Toxicology*, edited by Sir Mathew Reid, the President of the Royal College of Physicians, and one of the oldest members of the Buckingham, having been elected in mistake for somebody else; a *contretemps* that so enraged the Committee, that when the real man came up they black-balled him

---

contretemps: unfortunate incident

unanimously. Lord Arthur was a good deal puzzled at the technical terms used in both books, and had begun to regret that he had not paid more attention to his classics at Oxford, when in the second volume of Erskine, he found a very interesting and complete account of the properties of aconitine, written in fairly clear English. It seemed to him to be exactly the poison he wanted. It was swift - indeed, almost immediate, in its effect - perfectly painless, and when taken in the form of a gelatine capsule, the mode recommended by Sir Mathew, not by any means unpalatable. He accordingly made a note, upon his shirt-cuff, of the amount necessary for a fatal dose, put the books back in their places, and strolled up St. James's Street, to Pestle and Humbey's, the great chemists. Mr. Pestle, who always attended personally on the aristocracy,* was a good deal surprised at the order, and in a very **deferential** manner murmured something about a medical certificate being necessary. However, as soon as Lord Arthur explained to him that it was for a large Norwegian mastiff that he was obliged to get rid of, as it showed signs of **incipient** rabies, and had already bitten the coachman twice in the calf of the leg, he expressed himself as being perfectly satisfied, complimented Lord Arthur on his wonderful knowledge of Toxicology, and had the prescription made up immediately.

Lord Arthur put the capsule into a petty little silver

---

deferential: respectful

incipient: beginning

* the highest class in ceartain societies

bonbonnière that he saw in a shop window in Bond Street, threw away Pestle and Hambey's ugly pill-box, and drove off at once to Lady Clementina's.

"Well, *monsieur le mauvais sujet*," cried the old lady, as he entered the room, "why haven't you been to see me all this time?"

"My dear Lady Clem, I never have a moment to myself," said Lord Arthur, smiling.

"I suppose you mean that you go about all day long with Miss Sybil Merton, buying *chiffons* and talking nonsense? I cannot understand why people make such a fuss about being married. In my day we never dreamed of billing and cooing in public, or in private for that matter."

"I assure you I have not seen Sybil for twenty-four hours, Lady Clem. As far as I can make out, she belongs entirely to her milliners."

"Of course; that is the only reason you come to see an ugly old woman like myself. I wonder you men don't take warning. *On a fait des folies pour moi*, and here I am, a poor rheumatic creature, with a false front and a bad temper. Why, if it were not for dear Lady Jansen, who sends me all the worst French novels she can find, I don't think I could get through the day. Doctors

---

bonbonnière: (French) candy box

monsieur le mauvais sujet: (French) mister naughty

chiffons: (plural) thin, usually silk fabric

On a fait des folies pour moi: (French) People have behaved foolishly for my sake.

are no use at all, except to get fees out of one. They can't even cure my heartburn,"

"I have brought you a cure for that, Lady Clem," said Lord Arthur gravely. "It's a wonderful thing, invented by an American."

"I don't think I like American inventions, Arthur. I am quite sure I don't. I read some American novels lately, and they were quite nonsensical."

"Oh, but there is no nonsense at all about this, Lady Clem! I assure you it is a perfect cure. You must promise to try it"; and Lord Arthur brought the little box out of his pocket, and handed it to her.

"Well, the box is charming, Arthur. Is it really a present? That is very sweet of you. And is this the wonderful medicine? It looks like a *bonbon*. I'll take it at once."

"Good heavens! Lady Clem," cried Lord Arthur, catching hold of her hand, "you mustn't do anything of the kind. It is a homœopathic medicine, and if you take it without having heartburn, it might do you no end of harm. Wait till you have an attack, and take it then. You will be astonished at the result."

"I should like to take it now," said Lady Clementina, holding up to the light the little transparent capsule, with its floating bubble of liquid aconitine. "I am sure it is delicious. The fact is that, though I hate doctors, I love medicines. However, I'll keep it till my next attack."

"And when will that be?" asked Lord Arthur eagerly. "Will it

---

bonbon: candy

be soon?”

"I hope not for a week. I had a very bad time yesterday morning with it. But one never knows."

"You are sure to have one before the end of the month then, Lady Clem?"

"I am afraid so. But how sympathetic you are to-day, Arthur! Really, Sybil has done you a great deal of good. And now you must run away, for I am dining with some very dull people, who won't talk scandal, and I know that if I don't get my sleep now I shall never be able to keep awake during dinner. Good-bye, Arthur, give my love to Sybil, and thank you so much for the American medicine."

"You won't forget to take it, Lady Clem, will you?" said Lord Arthur, rising from his seat.

"Of course I won't, you silly boy. I think it is most kind of you to think of me, and I shall write and tell you if I want any more."

Lord Arthur left the house in high spirits, and with a feeling of immense relief.

That night he had an interview with Sybil Merton. He told her how he had been suddenly placed in a position of terrible difficulty, from which neither honour nor duty would allow him to recede. He told her that the marriage must be put off for the present, as until he had got rid of his fearful **entanglements**, he was not a free man. He implored her to trust him, and not to have any doubts about the future. Everything would come right, but

---

entanglements: difficult circumstances

patience was necessary.

The scene took place in the conservatory of Mr. Merton's house, in Park Lane, where Lord Arthur had dined as usual. Sybil had never seemed more happy, and for a moment Lord Arthur had been tempted to play the coward's part, to write to Lady Clementina for the pill, and to let the marriage go on as if there was no such person as Mr. Podgers in the world. His better nature, however, soon asserted itself, and even when Sybil flung herself weeping into his arms, he did not falter. The beauty that stirred his senses had touched his conscience also. He felt that to wreck so fair a life for the sake of a few months' pleasure would be a wrong thing to do.

He stayed with Sybil till nearly midnight, comforting her and being comforted in turn, and early the next morning he left for Venice, after writing a manly, firm letter to Mr. Merton about the necessary postponement of the marriage.

IV

In Venice he met his brother, Lord Surbiton, who happened to have come over from Corfu in his yacht. The two young men spent a delightful fortnight together. In the morning they rode on the Lido, or glided up and down the green canals in their long black gondola; in the afternoon they usually entertained visitors on the yacht; and in the evening they dined at Florian's, and smoked innumerable cigarettes on the Piazza. Yet somehow Lord Arthur was not happy. Every day he studied the obituary column in the *Times*, expecting to see a notice of Lady

Clementina's death, but every day he was disappointed. He began to be afraid that some accident had happened to her, and often regretted that he had prevented her taking the aconitine when she had been so anxious to try its effect. Sybil's letters, too, though full of love, and trust, and terderness, were often very sad in their tone, and sometimes he used to think that he was parted from her for ever.

After a fortnight Lord Surbiton got bored with Venice, and determined to run down the coast to Ravenna, as he heard that there was some capital cock-shooting in the Pinetum. Lord Arthur at first refused absolutely to come, but Surbiton, of whom he was extremely fond, finally persuaded him that if he stayed at Danielli's by himself he would be moped to death, and on the morning of the 15th they started, with a strong nor'east wind blowing, and a rather choppy sea. The sport was excellent, and the free, open-air life brought the colour back to Lord Arthur's cheek, but about the 22nd he became anxious about Lady Clementina, and, in spite of Surbiton's **remonstrances**, came back to Venice by train.

As he stepped out of his gondola on to the hotel steps, the proprietor came forward to meet him with a sheaf of telegrams. Lord Arthur snatched them out of his hand, and tore them open. Everything had been successful. Lady Clementina had died quite suddenly on the night of the 17th!

His first thought was for Sybil, and he sent her off a telegram announcing his immediate return to London. He then ordered his

---

remonstrances: protests

valet to pack his things for the night mail, sent his gondoliers about five times their proper fare, and ran up to his sitting-room with a light step and a buoyant heart. There he found three letters waiting for him. One was from Sybil herself, full of sympathy and condolence. The others were from his mother, and from Lady Clementina's solicitor. It seemed that the old lady had dined with the Duchess that very night, had delighted every one by her wit and *esprit*, but had gone home somewhat early, complaining of heartburn. In the morning she was found dead in her bed, having apparently suffered no pain. Sir Mathew Reid had been sent for at once, but, of course, there was nothing to be done, and she was to be buried on the 22nd at Beauchamp Chalcote. A few days before she died she had made her will, and left Lord Arthur her little house in Curzon Street, and all her furniture, personal effects, and pictures, with the exception of her collection of miniatures, which was to go to her sister, Lady Margaret Rufford, and her amethyst necklace, which Sybil Merton was to have. The property was not of much value; but Mr. Mansfield, the solicitor, was extremely anxious for Lord Arthur to return at once, if possible, as there were a great many bills to be paid, and Lady Clementina had never kept any regular accounts.

Lord Arthur was very much touched by Lady Clementina's kind remembrance of him, and felt that Mr. Podgers had a great deal to answer for. His love of Sybil, however, dominated every other emotion, and the consciousness that he had done his duty gave him peace and comfort. When he arrived at Charing Cross, he felt perfectly happy.

The Mertons received him very kindly. Sybil made him promise that he would never again allow anything to come between them, and the marriage was fixed for the 7th June. Life seemed to him once more bright and beautiful, and all his old gladness came back to him again.

One day, however, as he was going over the house in Curzon Street, in company with Lady Clementina's solicitor and Sybil herself, burning packages of faded letters, and turning out drawers of odd rubbish, the young girl suddenly gave a little cry of delight.

"What have you found, Sybil?" said Lord Arthur, looking up from his work, and smiling.

"This lovely little silver *bonbonnière*, Arthur. Isn't it quaint and Dutch? Do give it to me! I know amethysts won't become me till I am over eighty."

It was the box that had held the aconitine.

Lord Arthur started, and a faint blush came into his cheek. He had almost entirely forgotten what he had done, and it seemed to him a curious coincidence that Sybil, for whose sake he had gone through all that terrible anxiety, should have been the first to remind him of it.

"Of course you can have it, Sybil. I gave it to poor Lady Clem myself."

"Oh! thank you, Arthur; and may I have the *bonbon* too? I had no notion that Lady Clementina liked sweets. I thought she was far too intellectual."

Lord Arthur grew deadly pale, and a horrible idea crossed his mind.

"*Bonbon*, Sybil? What do you mean?" he said in a slow, hoarse voice.

"There is one in it, that is all. It looks quite old and dusty, and I have not the slightest intention of eating it. What is the matter, Arthur? How white you look!"

Lord Arthur rushed across the room, and seized the box. Inside it was the amber-coloured capsule, with its poison-bubble. Lady Clementina had died a natural death after all!

The shock of the discovery was almost too much for him. He flung the capsule into the fire, and sank on the sofa with a cry of despair.

V

Mr. Merton was a good deal distressed at the second postponement of the marriage, and Lady Julia, who had already ordered her dress for the wedding, did all in her power to make Sybil break off the match. Dearly, however, as Sybil loved her mother, she had given her whole life into Lord Arthur's hands, and nothing that Lady Julia could say could make her **waver** in her faith. As for Lord Arthur himself, it took him days to get over his terrible disappointment, and for a time his nerves were completely unstrung. His excellent common sense, however, soon asserted itself, and his sound, practical mind did not leave him long in doubt about what to do. Poison having proved a

---

waver: hesitate; be uncertain

complete failure, dynamite, or some other form of explosive, was obviously the proper thing to try.

He accordingly looked again over the list of his friends and relatives, and, after careful consideration, determined to blow up his uncle, the Dean of Chichester. The Dean, who was a man of great culture and learning, was extremely fond of clocks, and had a wonderful collection of timepieces, ranging from the fifteenth century to the present day, and it seemed to Lord Arthur that this hobby of the good Dean's offered him an excellent opportunity for carrying out his scheme. Where to **procure** an explosive machine was, of course, quite another matter. The London Directory gave him no information on the point, and he felt that there was very little use in going to Scotland Yard about it, as they never seemed to know anything about the movements of the dynamite faction till after an explosion had taken place, and not much even then.

Suddenly he thought of his friend Rouvaloff, a young Russian of very revolutionary tendencies, whom he had met at Lady Windermere's in the winter. Count Rouvaloff was supposed to be writing a life of Peter the Great, and to have come over to England for the purpose of studying the documents relating to that Tsar's residence in this country as a ship carpenter; but it was generally suspected that he was a Nihilist agent, and there was no doubt that the Russian Embassy did not look with any favour upon his presence in London. Lord Arthur felt that he was just the man for his purpose, and drove down one morning

---

procure: get

to his lodgings in Bloomsbury, to ask his advice and assistance.

"So you are taking up politics seriously?" said Count Rouvaloff, when Lord Arthur had told him the object of his mission; but Lord Arthur, who hated swagger of any kind, felt bound to admit to him that he had not the slightest interest in social questions, and simply wanted the explosive machine for a purely family matter, in which no one was concerned but himself.

Count Rouvaloff looked at him for some moments in amazement, and then seeing that he was quite serious, wrote an address on a piece of paper, initialled it, and handed it to him across the table.

"Scotland Yard would give a good deal to know this address, my dear fellow."

"They shan't have it," cried Lord Arthur, laughing; and after shaking the young Russian warmly by the hand he ran downstairs, examined the paper, and told the coachman to drive to Soho Square.

There he dismissed him, and strolled down Greek Street, till he came to a place called Bayle's Court. He passed under the archway, and found himself in a curious *cul-de-sac*, that was apparently occupied by a French laundry, as a perfect network of clothes-lines was stretched across from house to house, and there was a flutter of white linen in the morning air. He walked right to the end, and knocked at a little green house. After some delay, during which every window in the court became a blurred mass of peering faces, the door was opened by a rather rough-looking foreigner, who asked him in very bad English what his business was. Lord Arthur handed him the paper Count Rouvaloff had given him. When the man saw it he bowed, and invited Lord Arthur into a very shabby front parlour on the ground floor, and in a few moments Herr Winckelkopf, as he was called in England, bustled into the room, with a very wine-stained napkin round his neck, and a fork in his left hand.

"Count Rouvaloff has given me an introduction to you," said Lord Arthur, bowing, "and I am anxious to have a short interview with you on a matter of business. My name is Smith, Mr. Robert Smith, and I want you to supply me with an explosive clock."

"Charmed to meet you, Lord Arthur," said the genial little German, laughing. "Don't look so alarmed, it is my duty to know everybody, and I remember seeing you one evening at Lady Windermere's. I hope her ladyship is quite well. Do you mind sitting with me while I finish my breakfast? There is an excellent pâté, and my friends are kind enough to say that my Rhine wine is better than any they get at the German Embassy," and before Lord Arthur had got over his surprise at being recognised, he found himself seated in the back-room, sipping the most delicious Marcobrünner out of a pale yellow hock-glass marked with the Imperial monogram, and chatting in the friendliest manner possible to the famous conspirator.

"Explosive clocks," said Herr Winckelkopf, "are not very good things for foreign exportation, as, even if they succeed in passing the Custom House, the train service is so irregular, that they usually go off before they have reached their proper destination. If, however, you want one for home use, I can supply you with an excellent article, and guarantee that you will be satisfied with the result. May I ask for whom it is intended? If it is for the police, or for any one connected with Scotland Yard, I am afraid I cannot do anything for you. The English detectives are really our best friends, and I have always found that by relying on their stupidity, we can do exactly what we like. I could not spare one of them."

"I assure you," said Lord Arthur, "that it has nothing to do with the police at all. In fact, the clock is intended for the Dean of Chichester."

"Dear me! I had no idea that you felt so strongly about religion, Lord Arthur. Few young men do nowadays."

"I am afraid you overrate me, Herr Winckelkopf," said Lord Arthur, blushing. "The fact is, I really know nothing about theology."

"It is a purely private matter then?"

"Purely private."

Herr Winckelkopf shrugged his shoulders, and left the room, returning in a few minutes with a round cake of dynamite about the size of a penny, and a pretty little French clock, surmounted by an ormolu[1] figure of Liberty trampling on the hydra of Despotism.[2]

Lord Arthur's face brightened up when he saw it. "That is just what I want," he cried, "and now tell me how it goes off."

"Ah! there is my secret," answered Herr Winckelkopf, contemplating his invention with a justifiable look of pride; "let me know when you wish it to explode, and I will set the machine to the moment."

"Well, to-day is Tuesday, and if you could send it off at

1 an alloy covered in copper, zinc or tin

2 the exercise of power (cruel or oppressive way)

once -"

"That is impossible; I have a great deal of important work on hand for some friends of mine in Moscow. Still, I might send it off to-morrow."

"Oh, it will be quite time enough!" said Lord Arthur politely, "if it is delivered to-morrow night or Thursday morning. For the moment of the explosion, say Friday at noon exactly. The Dean is always at home at that hour."

"Friday, at noon," repeated Herr Winckelkopf, and he made a note to that effect in a large ledger that was lying on a bureau near the fireplace.

"And now," said Lord Arthur, rising from his seat, "pray let me know how much I am in your debt.'

"It is such a small matter, Lord Arthur, that I do not care to make any change. The dynamite comes to seven and sixpence, the clock will be three pounds ten, and the carriage about five shillings. I am only too pleased to oblige any friend of Count Rouvaloff's."

"But your trouble, Herr Winckelkopf?"

"Oh, that is nothing! It is a pleasure to me. I do not work for money; I live entirely for my art."

Lord Arthur laid down £4 2s. 6d. on the table, thanked the little German for his kindness, and, having succeeded in declining an invitation to meet some Anarchists at a meat-tea on the following Saturday, left the house and went off to the Park.

For the next two days he was in a state of the greatest excitement, and on Friday at twelve o'clock he drove down to the Buckingham to wait for news. All the afternoon the stolid hall-porter kept posting up telegrams from various parts of the country giving the results of horse-races, the verdicts in divorce suits, the state of the weather, and the like, while the tape ticked out wearisome details about an all-night sitting in the House of Commons, and a small panic on the Stock Exchange. At four o'clock the evening papers came in, and Lord Arthur disappeared into the library with the *Pall Mall*, the *St. James's*, the *Globe*, and the *Echo*, to the immense **indignation** of Colonel Goodchild, who wanted to read the reports of a speech he had delivered that morning at the Mansion House, on the subject of South African Missions, and the advisability of having black Bishops in every province, and for some reason or other had a strong prejudice against the *Evening News*. None of the papers, however, contained even the slightest allusion to Chichester, and Lord Arthur felt that the attempt must have failed. It was a terrible blow to him, and for a time he was quite unnerved. Herr Winckelkopf, whom he went to see the next day was full of elaborate apologies, and offered to supply him with another clock free of charge, or with a case of nitro-glycerine bombs at cost price. But he had lost all faith in explosives, and Herr Winckelkopf himself acknowledged that everything is so adulterated nowadays, that even dynamite can hardly be got in a pure condition. The little German, however, while admitting that something must have gone wrong with the machinery, was not without hope that the clock might still go off, and instanced the case of a barometer that he had once sent to the military

---

indignation: anger

Governor at Odessa, which, though timed to explode in ten days, had not done so for something like three months. It was quite true that when it did go off, it merely succeeded in blowing a housemaid to atoms, the Governor having gone out of town six weeks before, but at least it showed that dynamite, as a destructive force, was, when under the control of machinery, a powerful, though somewhat unpunctual agent. Lord Arthur was a little consoled by this reflection, but even here he was destined to disappointment, for two days afterwards, as he was going upstairs, the Duchess called him into her boudoir, and showed him a letter she had just received from the Deanery.

"Jane writes charming letters," said the Duchess; "you must really read her last. It is quite as good as the novels Mudie sends us."

Lord Arthur seized the letter from her hand. It ran as follows:-

THE DEANERY, CHICHESTER

27th May.

My Dearest Aunt,

Thank you so much for the flannel for the Dorcas Society, and also for the gingham. I quite agree with you that it is nonsense their wanting to wear pretty things, but everybody is so Radical and irreligious nowadays, that it is difficult to make them see that they should not try and dress like the upper classes. I am sure I don't know what we are coming to. As papa has often said in his sermons, we live in an age of unbelief.

We have had great fun over a clock that an unknown

admirer sent papa last Thursday. It arrived in a wooden box from London, carriage paid, and papa feels it must have been sent by some one who had read his remarkable sermon, "Is Licence Liberty?" for on the top of the clock was a figure of a woman, with what papa said was the cap of Liberty on her head. I didn't think it very becoming myself, but papa said it was historical, so I suppose it is all right. Parker unpacked it, and papa put it on the mantelpiece in the library, and we were all sitting there on Friday morning, when just as the clock struck twelve, we heard a whirring noise, a little puff of smoke came from the pedestal of the figure, and the goddess of Liberty fell off, and broke her nose on the fender! Maria was quite alarmed, but it looked so ridiculous, that James and I went off into fits of laughter, and even papa was amused. When we examined it, we found it was a sort of alarm clock, and that, if you set it to a particular hour, and put some gunpowder and a cap under a little hammer, it went off whenever you wanted. Papa said it must not remain in the library, as it made a noise, so Reggie carried it away to the schoolroom, and does nothing but have small explosions all day long. Do you think Arthur would like one for a wedding present? I suppose they are quite fashionable in London. Papa says they should do a great deal of good, as they show that Liberty can't last, but must fall down. Papa says Liberty was invented at the time of the French Revolution. How awful it seems!

I have now to go to the Dorcas, where I will read them your most instructive letter. How true, dear aunt, your idea is, that in their rank of life they should wear what is unbecoming. I must say it is absurd, their anxiety about dress, when there are so many more important things in this world, and in the next. I am so glad your flowered poplin turned out so well, and that your lace was not torn. I am wearing my yellow satin, that you so kindly gave me, at the Bishop's on Wednesday, and think it will look all right. Would you have bows or not? Jennings says that every one wears bows now, and that the underskirt should be frilled. Reggie has just had another explosion, and papa has ordered the clock to be sent to the stables. I don't think papa likes it so much as he did at first, though he is very flattered at being sent such a pretty and ingenious toy. It shows that people read his sermons, and profit by them.

Papa sends his love, in which James, and Reggie, and Maria all unite, and, hoping that Uncle Cecil's gout is better, believe me, dear aunt, ever your affectionate niece,

Jane Percy

PS.- Do tell me about the bows. Jennings insists they are the fashion.

Lord Arthur looked so serious and unhappy over the letter, that the Duchess went into fits of laughter.

"My dear Arthur," she cried, "I shall never show you a young lady's letter again! But what shall I say about the clock? I think it is a capital invention, and I should like to have one myself."

"I don't think much of them," said Lord Arthur, with a sad smile, and, after kissing his mother, he left the room.

When he got upstairs, he flung himself on the sofa, and his

eyes filled with tears. He had done his best to commit this murder, but on both occasions he had failed, and through no fault of his own. He had tried to do his duty, but it seemed as if Destiny herself had turned traitor. He was oppressed with the sense of the barrenness of good intentions, of the **futility** of trying to be fine. Perhaps it would be better to break off the marriage altogether. Sybil would suffer, it is true, but suffering could not really mar a nature so noble as hers. As for himself, what did it matter? There is always some war in which a man can die, some cause to which a man can give his life, and as life had no pleasure for him, so death had no terror. Let Destiny work out his doom. He would not stir to help her.

At half-past seven he dressed, and went down to the club. Surbiton was there with a party of young men, and he was obliged to dine with them. Their trivial conversation and idle jests did not interest him, and as soon as coffee was brought he left them, inventing some engagement in order to get away. As he was going out of the club, the hall-porter handed him a letter. It was from Herr Winckelkopf, asking him to call down the next evening, and look at an explosive umbrella, that went off as soon as it was opened. It was the very latest invention, and had just arrived from Geneva. He tore the letter up into fragments. He had made up his mind not to try any more experiments. Then he wandered down to the Thames Embankment, and sat for hours by the river. The moon peered through a mane of tawny clouds, as if it were a lion's eye, and innumerable stars spangled the

---

futility: worthlessness; pointlessness

hollow vault, like gold dust powdered on a purple dome. Now and then a barge swung out into the turbid stream, and floated away with the tide, and the railway signals changed from green to scarlet as the trains ran shrieking across the bridge. After some time, twelve o'clock boomed from the tall tower at Westminster, and at each stroke of the sonorous bell the night seemed to tremble. Then the railway lights went out, one solitary lamp left gleaming like a large ruby on a giant mast, and the roar of the city became fainter.

At two o'clock he got up, and strolled towards Blackfriars. How unreal everything looked! How like a strange dream! The houses on the other side of the river seemed built out of darkness. One would have said that silver and shadow had fashioned the world anew. The huge dome of St. Paul's loomed like a bubble through the dusky air.

As he approached Cleopatra's Needle he saw a man leaning over the parapet, and as he came nearer the man looked up, the gas-light falling full upon kis face.

It was Mr. Podgers, the chiromantist! No one could mistake the fat, flabby face, the gold-rimmed spectacles, the sickly feeble smile, the sensual mouth.

Lord Arthur stopped. A brilliant idea flashed across him, and he stole softly up behind. In a moment he had seized Mr. Podgers by the legs, and flung him into the Thames. There was a coarse oath, a heavy splash, and all was still. Lord Arthur looked anxiously over, but could see nothing of the chiromantist but a tall hat, pirouetting in an eddy of moonlit water. After a time it also sank, and no trace of Mr. Podgers was visible. Once he thought that he caught sight of the bulky misshapen figure striking out for the staircase by the bridge, and a horrible feeling of failure came over him, but it turned out to be merely a reflection, and when the moon shone out from behind a cloud it passed away. At last he seemed to have realised the **decree** of Destiny. He heaved a deep sigh of relief, and Sybil's name came to his lips.

"Have you dropped anything, sir?" said a voice behind him suddenly.

He turned round, and saw a policeman with a bull's-eye lantern.

"Nothing of importance, sergeant," he answered, smiling, and hailing a passing hansom, he jumped in, and told the man to drive to Belgrave Square.

For the next few days he alternated between hope and fear. There were moments when he almost expected Mr. Podgers to walk into the room, and yet at other times he felt that Fate could not be so unjust to him. Twice he went to the chiromantist's address in West Moon Street, but he could not bring himself to ring the bell. He longed for certainty, and was afraid of it.

Finally it came. He was sitting in the smoking-room of the club having tea, and listening rather wearily to Surbiton's account of the last comic song at the Gaiety, when the waiter came in with the evening papers. He took up the *St. James's*, and was **listlessly** turning over its pages, when this strange heading

---

decree: order

listlessly: casually

caught his eye:

"SUICIDE OF A CHIROMANTIST."

He turned pale with excitement, and began to read. The paragraph ran as follows:

Yesterday morning, at seven o'clock, the body of Mr. Septimus R. Podgers, the eminent chiromantist, was washed on shore at Greenwich, just in front of the Ship Hotel. The unfortunate gentleman had been missing for some days, and considerable anxiety for his safety had been felt in chiromantic circles. It is supposed that he committed suicide under the influence of a temporary mental derangement, caused by overwork, and a verdict to that effect was returned this afternoon by the coroner's jury. Mr. Podgers had just completed an elaborate treatise on the subject of the Human Hand, that will shortly be published, when it will no doubt attract much attention. The deceased was sixty-five years of age, and does not seem to have left any relations.

Lord Arthur rushed out of the club with the paper still in his hand, to the immense amazement of the hall-porter, who tried in vain to stop him, and drove at once to Park Lane. Sybil saw him from the window, and something told her that he was the bearer of good news. She ran down to meet him, and, when she saw his face, she knew that all was well.

"My dear Sybil," cried Lord Arthur, "let us be married to-morrow!"

"You foolish boy! Why, the cake is not even ordered!" said Sybil, laughing through her tears.

VI

When the wedding took place, some three weeks later, St. Peter's was crowded with a perfect mob of smart people. The service was read in the most impressive manner by the Dean of Chichester, and everybody agreed that they had never seen a handsomer couple than the bride and bridegroom. They were more than handsome, however - they were happy. Never for a single moment did Lord Arthur regret all that he had suffered for Sybil's sake, while she, on her side, gave him the best things a woman can give to any man - worship, tenderness, and love. For them romance was not killed by reality. They always felt young.

Some years afterwards, when two beautiful children had been born to them, Lady Windermere came down on a visit to Alton Priory, a lovely old place, that had been the Duke's wedding present to his son; and one afternoon as she was sitting with Lady Arthur under a lime-tree in the garden, watching the little boy and girl as they played up and down the rose-walk, like fitful sunbeams, she suddenly took her hostess's hand in hers, and said, "Are you happy, Sybil?"

"Dear Lady Windermere, of course I am happy. Aren't you?"

"I have no time to be happy, Sybil. I always like the last person who is introduced to me; but, as a rule, as soon as I know people I get tired of them."

"Don't your lions satisfy you, Lady Windermere?"

"Oh dear, no! lions are only good for one season. As soon as their manes are cut, they are the dullest creatures going. Besides, they behave very badly, if you are really nice to them. Do you remember that horrid Mr. Podgers? He was a dreadful **imposter**. Of course, I didn't mind that at all, and even when he wanted to borrow money I forgave him, but I could not stand his making love to me. He has really made me hate chiromancy. I go in for telepathy now. It is much more amusing."

"You mustn't say anything against chiromancy here, Lady Windermere; it is the only subject that Arthur does not like people to chaff* about. I assure you he is quite serious over it."

"You don't mean to say that he believes in it, Sybil?"

"Ask him, Lady Windermere, here he is"; and Lord Arthur came up the garden with a large bunch of yellow roses in his hand, and his two children dancing round him.

"Lord Arthur?"

"Yes, Lady Windermere."

"You don't mean to say that you believe in chiromancy?"

"Of course I do," said the young man, smiling.

"But why?"

"Because I owe to it all the happiness of my life," he murmured, throwing himself into a wicker chair.

"My dear Lord Arthur, what do you owe to it?"

"Sybil," he answered, handing his wife the roses, and

---

imposter: fake; phony

* tease

looking into her violet eyes.

"What nonsense!" cried Lady Windermere. "I never heard such nonsense in all my life."

Did Podgers just make it up?

Why did Arthur believe him?

Watson = MC/N

The Red-Headed League

1st POV

I had called upon my friend, Mr. Sherlock Holmes, one day in the autumn of last year and found him in deep conversation with a very stout, florid-faced, elderly gentleman with fiery red hair. With an apology for my intrusion, I was about to withdraw when Holmes pulled me **abruptly** into the room and closed the door behind me.

"You could not possibly have come at a better time, my dear Watson," he said **cordially**.

"I was afraid that you were engaged."

"So I am. Very much so."

"Then I can wait in the next room."

"Not at all. This gentleman, Mr. Wilson, has been my partner and helper in many of my most successful cases, and I have no doubt that he will be of the utmost use to me in yours also."

The stout gentleman half rose from his chair and gave a bob of greeting, with a quick little questioning glance from his small fat-encircled eyes.

"Try the settee," said Holmes, relapsing into his armchair and putting his fingertips together, as was his custom when in **judicial** moods. "I know, my dear Watson, that you share my

---

abruptly: suddenly

cordially: in a friendly way

judicial: critical

florid: having a red complexion

settee: a long seat made for more than one person

love of all that is **bizarre** and outside the conventions and humdrum routine of everyday life. You have shown your **relish** for it by the enthusiasm which has prompted you to chronicle, and, if you will excuse my saying so, somewhat to **embellish** so many of my own little adventures."

"Your cases have indeed been of the greatest interest to me," I observed.

"You will remember that I remarked the other day, just before we went into the very simple problem presented by Miss Mary Sutherland, that for strange effects and extraordinary combinations we must go to life itself, which is always far more daring than any effort of the imagination."

"A proposition which I took the liberty of doubting."

"You did, Doctor, but none the less you must come round to my view, for otherwise I shall keep on piling fact upon fact on you until your reason breaks down under them and **acknowledges** me to be right. Now, Mr. Jabez Wilson here has been good enough to call upon me this morning, and to begin a narrative which promises to be one of the most **singular** which I have listened to for some time. You have heard me remark that the strangest and most unique things are very often connected not with the larger but with the smaller crimes, and occasionally,

---

bizarre: odd

relish: liking; appreciation

embellish: enrich; enhance

acknowledges: accepts

singular: unique

indeed, where there is room for doubt whether any positive crime has been committed. As far as I have heard, it is impossible for me to say whether the present case is an instance of crime or not, but the course of events is certainly among the most singular that I have ever listened to. Perhaps, Mr. Wilson, you would have the great kindness to **recommence** your narrative. I ask you not merely because my friend Dr. Watson has not heard the opening part but also because the peculiar nature of the story makes me anxious to have every possible detail from your lips. As a rule, when I have heard some slight indication of the course of events, I am able to guide myself by the thousands of other similar cases which occur to my memory. In the present instance I am forced to admit that the facts are, to the best of my belief, unique."

The portly client puffed out his chest with an appearance of some little pride and pulled a dirty and wrinkled newspaper from the inside pocket of his greatcoat. As he glanced down the advertisement column, with his head thrust forward and the paper flattened out upon his knee, I took a good look at the man and endeavoured, after the fashion of my companion, to read the indications which might be presented by his dress or appearance.

I did not gain very much, however, by my inspection. Our visitor bore every mark of being an average commonplace British tradesman, obese, **pompous**, and slow. He wore rather baggy grey shepherd's check trousers, a not over-clean black frock-coat, unbuttoned in the front, and a drab waistcoat with a

---

recommence: start again

pompous: arrogant; self-important

heavy brassy Albert chain, and a square pierced bit of metal dangling down as an ornament. A frayed top-hat and a faded brown overcoat with a wrinkled velvet collar lay upon a chair beside him. Altogether, look as I would, there was nothing remarkable about the man save his blazing red head, and the expression of extreme **chagrin** and discontent upon his features.

Sherlock Holmes' quick eye took in my occupation, and he shook his head with a smile as he noticed my questioning glances. "Beyond the obvious facts that he has at some time done manual labour, that he takes snuff, that he is a Freemason, that he has been in China, and that he has done a considerable amount of writing lately, I can **deduce** nothing else."

Mr. Jabez Wilson started up in his chair, with his forefinger upon the paper, but his eyes upon my companion.

"How, in the name of good-fortune, did you know all that, Mr. Holmes?" he asked. "How did you know, for example, that I did manual labour? It's as true as gospel, for I began as a ship's carpenter."

"Your hands, my dear sir. Your right hand is quite a size larger than your left. You have worked with it, and the muscles are more developed."

"Well, the snuff, then, and the Freemasonry?"

"I won't insult your intelligence by telling you how I read that, especially as, rather against the strict rules of your order, you use an arc-and-compass breastpin."

---

chagrin: irritation

deduce: conclude; infer

"Ah, of course, I forgot that. But the writing?"

"What else can be indicated by that right cuff so very shiny for five inches, and the left one with the smooth patch near the elbow where you rest it upon the desk?"

"Well, but China?"

"The fish that you have tattooed immediately above your right wrist could only have been done in China. I have made a small study of tattoo marks and have even contributed to the literature of the subject. That trick of staining the fishes' scales of a delicate pink is quite peculiar to China. When, in addition, I see a Chinese coin hanging from your watch-chain, the matter becomes even more simple."

Mr. Jabez Wilson laughed heavily. "Well, I never!" said he. "I thought at first that you had done something clever, but I see that there was nothing in it after all."

"I begin to think, Watson," said Holmes, "that I make a mistake in explaining. '*Omne ignotum pro magnifico*,' you know, and my poor little reputation, such as it is, will suffer shipwreck if I am so **candid**. Can you not find the advertisement, Mr. Wilson?"

"Yes, I have got it now," he answered with his thick red finger planted halfway down the column. "Here it is. This is what began it all. You just read it for yourself, sir."

I took the paper from him and read as follows:

Omne ignotum pro magnifico: (Latin) Everything unknown is considered to be magnificent.

candid: honest

TO THE RED-HEADED LEAGUE: On account of the **bequest** of the late Ezekiah Hopkins, of Lebanon, Pennsylvania, U.S.A., there is now another vacancy open which **entitles** a member of the League to a salary of £4 a week for purely **nominal** services. All red-headed men who are sound in body and mind, and above the age of twenty-one years, are **eligible**. Apply in person on Monday, at eleven o'clock, to Duncan Ross, at the offices of the League, 7 Pope's Court, Fleet Street.

"What on earth does this mean?" I ejaculated after I had twice read over the extraordinary announcement.

Holmes chuckled and wriggled in his chair, as was his habit when in high spirits. "It is a little off the beaten track, isn't it?" said he. "And now, Mr. Wilson, off you go at scratch and tell us all about yourself, your household, and the effect which this advertisement had upon your fortunes. You will first make a note, Doctor, of the paper and the date."

"It is *The Morning Chronicle* of April 27, 1890. Just two months ago."

"Very good. Now, Mr. Wilson?"

"Well, it is just as I have been telling you, Mr. Sherlock Holmes," said Jabez Wilson, mopping his forehead; "I have a small pawnbroker's business at Coburg Square, near the City. It's

---

bequest: act of leaving by will; legacy

entitles: gives the right to

nominal: small; minimal

eligible: suitable

not a very large affair, and of late years it has not done more than just give me a living. I used to be able to keep two assistants, but now I only keep one; and I would have a job to pay him but that he is willing to come for half wages so as to learn the business."

"What is the name of this obliging youth?" asked Sherlock Holmes.

"His name is Vincent Spaulding, and he's not such a youth, either. It's hard to say his age. I should not wish a smarter assistant, Mr. Holmes; and I know very well that he could better himself and earn twice what I am able to give him. But, after all, if he is satisfied, why should I put ideas in his head?"

"Why, indeed? You seem most fortunate in having an employee who comes under the full market price. It is not a common experience among employers in this age. I don't know that your assistant is not as remarkable as your advertisement."

"Oh, he has his faults, too," said Mr. Wilson. "Never was such a fellow for photography. Snapping away with a camera when he ought to be improving his mind, and then diving down into the cellar like a rabbit into its hole to develop his pictures. That is his main fault, but on the whole he's a good worker. There's no **vice** in him."

"He is still with you, I presume?"

"Yes, sir. He and a girl of fourteen, who does a bit of simple cooking and keeps the place clean – that's all I have in the house, for I am a widower and never had any family. We live very quietly, sir, the three of us; and we keep a roof over our

---

vice: evil

heads and pay our debts, if we do nothing more.

"The first thing that put us out was that advertisement. Spaulding, he came down into the office just this day eight weeks, with this very paper in his hand, and he says:

" 'I wish to the Lord, Mr. Wilson, that I was a red-headed man.'

" 'Why that?' I asks.

" 'Why,' says he, 'here's another vacancy on the League of the Red-headed Men. It's worth quite a little fortune to any man who gets it, and I understand that there are more vacancies than there are men, so that the trustees are at their wits' end what to do with the money. If my hair would only change colour, here's a nice little crib all ready for me to step into.'

" 'Why, what is it, then?' I asked. You see, Mr. Holmes, I am a very stay-at-home man, and as my business came to me instead of my having to go to it, I was often weeks on end without putting my foot over the door-mat. In that way I didn't know much of what was going on outside, and I was always glad of a bit of news.

" 'Have you never heard of the League of the Red-headed Men?' he asked with his eyes open.

" 'Never.'

" 'Why, I wonder at that, for you are eligible yourself for one of the vacancies.'

" 'And what are they worth?' I asked.

" 'Oh, merely a couple of hundred a year, but the work is slight, and it need not interfere very much with one's other occupations.'

"Well, you can easily think that that made me prick up my ears, for the business has not been over-good for some years, and an extra couple of hundred would have been very handy.

" 'Tell me all about it,' said I.

" 'Well,' said he, showing me the advertisement, 'you can see for yourself that the League has a vacancy, and there is the address where you should apply for particulars. As far as I can make out, the League was founded by an American millionaire, Ezekiah Hopkins, who was very peculiar in his ways. He was himself red-headed, and he had a great sympathy for all red-headed men; so, when he died it was found that he had left his enormous fortune in the hands of trustees, with instructions to apply the interest to the providing of easy berths to men whose hair is of that colour. From all I hear it is splendid pay and very little to do.'

" 'But,' said I, 'there would be millions of red-headed men who would apply.'

" 'Not so many as you might think,' he answered. 'You see it is really confined to Londoners, and to grown men. This American had started from London when he was young, and he wanted to do the old town a good turn. Then, again, I have heard it is no use your applying if your hair is light red, or dark red, or anything but real bright, blazing, fiery red. Now, if you cared to apply, Mr. Wilson, you would just walk in; but perhaps it would hardly be worth your while to put yourself out of the way for the sake of a few hundred pounds.'

"Now, it is a fact, gentlemen, as you may see for yourselves, that my hair is of a very full and rich tint, so that it seemed to me that if there was to be any competition in the matter I stood as good a chance as any man that I had ever met. Vincent Spaulding seemed to know so much about it that I thought he might prove useful, so I just ordered him to put up the shutters for the day and to come right away with me. He was very willing to have a holiday, so we shut the business up and started off for the address that was given us in the advertisement.

"I never hope to see such a sight as that again, Mr. Holmes. From north, south, east, and west every man who had a shade of red in his hair had tramped into the city to answer the advertisement. Fleet Street was choked with red-headed folk, and Pope's Court looked like a coster's orange barrow. I should not have thought there were so many in the whole country as were brought together by that single advertisement. Every shade of colour they were – straw, lemon, orange, brick, Irish-setter, liver, clay; but, as Spaulding said, there were not many who had the real vivid flame-coloured tint. When I saw how many were waiting, I would have given it up in despair; but Spaulding would not hear of it. How he did it I could not imagine, but he pushed and pulled and butted until he got me through the crowd, and right up to the steps which led to the office. There was a double stream upon the stair, some going up in hope, and some coming back **dejected**; but we wedged in as well as we could and soon found ourselves in the office."

"Your experience has been a most entertaining one," remarked Holmes as his client paused and refreshed his memory

---

dejected: sad

with a huge pinch of snuff. "Pray continue your very interesting statement."

"There was nothing in the office but a couple wooden chairs and a deal table, behind which sat a small man with a head that was even redder than mine. He said a few words to each candidate as he came up, and then he always managed to find some fault in them which would **disqualify** them. Getting a vacancy did not seem to be such a very easy matter, after all. However, when our turn came the little man was much more favourable to me than to any of the others, and he closed the door as we entered, so that he might have a private word with us.

" 'This is Mr. Jabez Wilson,' said my assistant, 'and he is willing to fill a vacancy in the League.'

" 'And he is admirably suited for it,' the other answered. 'He has every requirement. I cannot recall when I have seen anything so fine.' He took a step backward, cocked his head on one side, and gazed at my hair until I felt quite **bashful**. Then suddenly he plunged forward, wrung my hand, and congratulated me warmly on my success.

" 'It would be injustice to hesitate,' said he. 'You will, however, I am sure, excuse me for taking an obvious precaution.' With that he seized my hair in both his hands, and tugged until I yelled with the pain. 'There is water in your eyes,' said he as he released me. 'I perceive that all is as it should be. But we have to be careful, for we have twice been deceived by wigs and once by

---

disqualify: exclude

bashful: embarrassed; shy

paint. I could tell you tales of cobbler's wax which would disgust you with human nature.' He stepped over to the window and shouted through it at the top of his voice that the vacancy was filled. A groan of disappointment came up from below, and the folk all trooped away in different directions until there was not a red-head to be seen except my own and that of the manager.

" 'My name,' said he, 'is Mr. Duncan Ross, and I am myself one of the pensioners upon the fund left by our noble **benefactor**. Are you a married man, Mr. Wilson? Have you a family?'

"I answered that I had not.

"His face fell immediately.

" 'Dear me!' he said gravely, 'that is very serious indeed! I am sorry to hear you say that. The fund was, of course, for the **propagation** and spread of the red-heads as well as for their maintenance. It is exceedingly unfortunate that you should be a bachelor.'

"My face lengthened at this, Mr. Holmes, for I thought that I was not to have the vacancy after all; but after thinking it over for a few minutes he said that it would be all right.

" 'In the case of another,' said he, 'the objection might be fatal, but we must stretch a point in favour of a man with such a head of hair as yours. When shall you be able to enter upon your new duties?'

" 'Well, it is a little awkward, for I have a business already,' said I.

---

benefactor: person who gives financial aid

propagation: reproduction

" 'Oh, never mind about that, Mr. Wilson!' said Vincent Spaulding. 'I should be able to look after that for you.'

" 'What would be the hours?' I asked.

" 'Ten to two.'

"Now a pawnbroker's business is mostly done of an evening, Mr. Holmes, especially Thursday and Friday evening, which is just before pay-day; so it would suit me very well to earn a little in the mornings. Besides, I knew that my assistant was a good man, and that he would see to anything that turned up.

" 'That would suit me very well,' said I. 'And the pay?'

" 'Is £4 a week.'

" 'And the work?'

" 'Is purely nominal.'

" 'What do you call purely nominal?'

" 'Well, you have to be in the office, or at least in the building, the whole time. If you leave, you **forfeit** your whole position forever. The will is very clear upon that point. You don't **comply** with the conditions if you budge from the office during that time.'

" 'It's only four hours a day, and I should not think of leaving ,' said I.

" 'No excuse will avail,' said Mr. Duncan Ross; 'neither sickness nor business nor anything else. There you must stay, or you lose your billet.'

" 'And the work?'

---

forfeit: lose

comply: do as required

avail: help

billet: a place where soldiers are kept temporarily

" 'Is to copy out the *Encyclopaedia Britannica*. There is the first volume of it in that press. You must find your own ink, pens, and blotting-paper, but we provide this table and chair. Will you be ready to-morrow?'

" 'Certainly,' I answered.

" 'Then, good-bye, Mr. Jabez Wilson, and let me congratulate you once more on the important position which you have been fortunate enough to gain.' He bowed me out of the room, and I went home with my assistant, hardly knowing what to say or do, I was so pleased at my own good fortune.

"Well, I thought over the matter all day, and by evening I was in low spirits again; for I had quite persuaded myself that the whole affair must be some great hoax or fraud, though what its object might be I could not imagine. It seemed altogether past belief that anyone could make such a will, or that they would pay such a sum for doing anything so simple as copying out the *Encyclopaedia Britannica.* Vincent Spaulding did what he could to cheer me up, but by bedtime I had reasoned myself out of the whole thing. However, in the morning I determined to have a look at it anyhow, so I bought a penny bottle of ink, and with a quill-pen, and seven sheets of foolscap paper, I started off for Pope's Court.

"Well, to my surprise and delight, everything was as right as possible. The table was set out ready for me, and Mr. Duncan Ross was there to see that I got fairly to work. He started me off upon the letter A, and then he left me; but he would drop in from time to time to see that all was right with me. At two o'clock he bade me good-day, complimented me upon the amount that I had written, and locked the door of the office after me.

"This went on day after day, Mr. Holmes, and on Saturday the manager came in and planked down four golden sovereigns for my week's work. It was the same next week, and the same the week after. Every morning I was there at ten, and every afternoon I left at two. By degrees Mr. Duncan Ross took to coming in only once of a morning, and then, after a time, he did not come in at all. Still, of course, I never dared to leave the room for an instant, for I was not sure when he might come, and the billet was such a good one, and suited me so well, that I would not risk the loss of it.

"Eight weeks passed away like this, and I had written about Abbots and Archery and Armour and Architecture and Attica, and hoped with **diligence** that I might get on to the B's before very long. It cost me something in foolscap, and I had pretty nearly filled a shelf with my writings. And then suddenly the whole business came to an end."

"To an end?"

"Yes, sir. And no later than this morning. I went to my work as usual at ten o'clock, but the door was shut and locked, with a little square of cardboard hammered on to the middle of the panel with a tack. Here it is, and you can read for youeself."

He held up a piece of white cardboard about the size of a sheet of note-paper. It read in this fashion:

---

diligence: hard work

foolscap: a piece of paper (13 x 8)

THE RED-HEADED LEAGUE

IS

DISSOLVED

October 9, 1890

Sherlock Holmes and I surveyed this curt announcement and the **rueful** face behind it, until the comical side of the affair so completely overtopped every other consideration that we both burst out into a roar of laughter.

"I cannot see that there is anything very funny," cried our client, flushing up to the roots of his flaming head. "If you can do nothing better than laugh at me, I can go elsewhere."

"No, no," cried Holmes, shoving him back into the chair from which he had half risen. "I really wouldn't miss your case for the world. It is most refreshingly unusual. But there is, if you will excuse my saying so, something just a little funny about it. Pray what steps did you take when you found the card upon the door?"

"I was **staggered**, sir. I did not know what to do. Then I called at the offices round, but none of them seemed to know anything about it. Finally, I went to the landlord, who is an accountant living on the ground floor, and I asked him if he could tell me what had become of the Red-headed League. He said that he had never heard of any such body.Then I asked him

---

dissolved: came to an end

rueful: sorrowful

staggered: shocked

curt: rudely brief

who Mr. Duncan Ross was. He answered that the name was to him.

" 'Well,' said I, 'the gentleman at No. 4.'

" 'What, the red-headed man?'

" 'Yes.'

" 'Oh,' said he, 'his name was William Morris. He was a solicitor and was using my room as a temporary convenience until his new premises were ready. He moved out yesterday.'

" 'Where could I find him?'

" 'Oh, at his new offices. He did tell me the address. Yes, 17 King Edward Street, near St. Paul's.'

"I started off, Mr. Holmes, but when I got to that address it was a manufactory of artificial knee-caps, and no one in it had ever heard of either Mr. William Morris or Mr. Duncan Ross."

"And what did you do then?" asked Holmes.

"I went home to Saxe-Coburg Square, and I took the advice of my assistant. But he could not help me in any way. He could only say that if I waited I should hear by post. But that was not quite good enough, Mr. Holmes. I did not wish to lose such a place without a struggle, so, as I had heard that you were good enough to give advice to poor folk who were in need of it, I came right away to you."

"And you did very wisely," said Holmes. "Your case is an exceedingly remarkable one, and I shall be happy to look into it. From what you have told me I think that it is possible that graver issues hang from it than might at first sight appear."

"Grave enough!" said Mr. Jabez Wilson. "Why, I have lost four pound a week."

solicitor: a legal professional

"As far as you are personally concerned," remarked Holmes, "I do not see that you have any grievance against this extraordinary league. On the contrary, you are, as I understand, richer by some £30, to say nothing of the minute knowledge which you have gained on every subject which comes under the letter A. You have lost nothing by them."

"No, sir. But I want to find out about them, and who they are, and what their object was in playing this **prank** - if it was a prank - upon me. It was a pretty expensive joke for them, for it cost them two and thirty pounds."

"We shall endeavour to clear up these points for you. And, first, one or two questions, Mr. Wilson. This assistant of yours who first called your attention to the advertisement – how long had he been with you?"

"About a month then."

"How did he come?"

"In answer to an advertisement."

"Was he the only applicant?"

"No, I had a dozen."

"Why did you pick him?"

"Because he was handy and would come cheap."

"At half wages, in fact."

"Yes."

"What is he like, this Vincent Spaulding?"

"Small, stout-built, very quick in his ways, no hair on his face, though he's not short of thirty. Has a white splash of acid

---

prank: trick

upon his forehead."

Holmes sat up in his chair in considerable excitement. "I thought as much," said he. "Have you ever observed that his ears are pierced for earrings?"

"Yes, sir. He told me that a gipsy had done it for him when he was a lad."

"Hum!" said Holmes, sinking back in deep thought. "He is still with you?"

"Oh, yes, sir; I have only just left him."

"And has your business been attended to in your absence?"

"Nothing to complain of, sir. There's never very much to do of a morning."

"That will do, Mr. Wilson. I shall be happy to give you an opinion upon the subject in the course of a day or two. To-day is Saturday, and I hope that by Monday we may come to a conclusion."

"Well, Watson," said Holmes when our visitor had left us, "what do you make of it all?"

"I make nothing of it," I answered frankly. "It is a most mysterious business."

"As a rule," said Holmes, "the more bizarre a thing is the less mysterious it proves to be. It is your commonplace, featureless crimes which are really puzzling, just as a commonplace face is the most difficult to identify. But I must be prompt over this matter."

"What are you going to do, then?" I asked.

"To smoke," he answered. "It is quite a three pipe problem, and I beg that you won't speak to me for fifty minutes." He curled himself up in his chair, with his thin knees drawn up to his hawk-like nose, and there he sat with his eyes closed and his black clay pipe thrusting out like the bill of some strange bird. I had come to the conclusion that he had dropped asleep, and indeed was nodding myself, when he suddenly sprang out of his chair with the gesture of a man who has made up his mind and put his pipe down upon the mantelpiece.

"Sarasate plays at the St. James's Hall this afternoon," he remarked. "What do you think, Watson? Could your patients spare you for a few hours?"

"I have nothing to do to-day. My practice is never very absorbing."

"Then put on your hat and come. I am going through the City first, and we can have some lunch on the way. I observe that there is a good deal of German music on the programme, which is rather more to my taste than Italian or French. It is introspective, and I want to introspect. Come along!"

We travelled by the Underground as far as Aldersgate; and a short walk took us to Saxe-Coburg Square, the scene of the singular story which we had listened to in the morning. It was a poky, little, shabby-genteel place, where four lines of dingy two-storied brick houses looked out into a small railed-in enclosure, where a lawn of weedy grass and a few clumps of faded laurel bushes made a hard fight against a smoke-laden and uncongenial atmosphere. Three gilt balls and a brown board with "JABEZ WILSON" in white letters, upon a corner house, announced the place where our red-headed client carried on his business. Sherlock Holmes stopped in front of it with his head on one side and looked it all over, with his eyes shining brightly between puckered lids. Then he walked slowly up the street, and then down again to the corner, still looking keenly at the houses. Finally he returned to the pawnbroker's, and, having thumped vigorously upon the pavement with his stick two or three times, he went up to the door and knocked. It was instantly opened by a bright-looking, clean-shaven young fellow, who asked him to step in.

"Thank you," said Holmes, "I only wished to ask you how you would go from here to the Strand."

"Third right, fourth left," answered the assistant promptly, closing the door.

"Smart fellow, that," observed Holmes as he walked away. "He is, in my judgment, the fourth smartest man in London, and for daring I am not sure that he has not a claim to be third. I have known something of him before."

"**Evidently**," said I, "Mr. Wilson's assistant counts for a good deal in this mystery of the Red-headed League. I am sure that you inquired your way merely in order that you might see him."

"Not him."

"What then?"

"The knees of his trousers."

"And what did you see?"

"What I expected to see."

"Why did you beat the pavement?"

---

evidently: clearly

"My dear doctor, this is a time for observation, not for talk. We are spies in an enemy's country. We know something of Saxe-Coburg Square. Let us now explore the parts which lie behind it."

The road in which we found ourselves as we turned round the corner from the retired Saxe-Coburg Square presented as great a contrast to it as the front of a picture does to the back. It was one of the main arteries which conveyed the traffic of the City to the north and west. The roadway was blocked with the immense stream of commerce flowing in a double tide inward and outward, while the footpaths were black with the hurrying swarm of pedestrians. It was difficult to realize as we looked at the line of fine shops and stately business premises that they really **abutted** on the other side upon the faded and stagnant square which we had just quitted.

"Let me see," said Holmes, standing at the corner and glancing along the line, "I should like just to remember the order of the houses here. It is a hobby of mine to have an exact knowledge of London. There is Mortimer's, the tobacconist, the little newspaper shop, the Coburg branch of the City and Suburban Bank, the Vegetarian Restaurant, and McFarlane's carriage-building depot. That carries us right on to the other block. And now, Doctor, we've done our work, so it's time we had some play. A sandwich and a cup of coffee, and then off to violin-land, where all is sweetness and delicacy and harmony, and there are no red-headed clients to vex us with their

---

abutted: bordered

conundrums."

My friend was an enthusiastic musician, being himself not only a very capable performer but a composer of no ordinary merit. All the afternoon he sat in the stalls wrapped in the most perfect happiness, gently waving his long, thin fingers in time to the music, while his gently smiling face and his **languid**, dreamy eyes were unlike those of Holmes, the sleuth-hound, Holmes the relentless, keen-witted, ready-handed criminal agent, as it was possible to **conceive**. In his singular character the dual nature alternately asserted itself, and his extreme exactness and **astuteness** represented, as I have often thought, the reaction against the poetic and contemplative mood which occasionally predominated in him. The swing of his nature took him from extreme languor to devouring energy; and, as I knew well, he was never so truly formidable as when, for days on end, he had been lounging in his armchair amid his improvisations and his black-letter editions. Then it was that the lust of the chase would suddenly come upon him, and that his brilliant reasoning power would rise to the level of intuition, until those who were unacquainted with his methods would look askance at him as on a man whose knowledge was not that of other mortals. When I saw him that afternoon so enwrapped in the music at St. James's Hall I felt that an evil time might be coming upon those whom

---

conundrums: puzzles

languid: lazy, dull

conceive: imagine

astuteness: shrewdness

he had set himself to hunt down.

"You want to go home, no doubt, Doctor," he remarked as we emerged.

"Yes, it would be as well."

"And I have some business to do which will take some hours. This business at Coburg Square is serious."

"Why serious?"

"A considerable crime is in contemplation. I have every reason to believe that we shall be in time to stop it. But to-day being Saturday rather complicates matters. I shall want your help to-night."

"At what time?"

"Ten will be early enough."

"I shall be at Baker Street at ten."

"Very well. And, I say, Doctor, there may be some little danger, so kindly put your army revolver in your pocket." He waved his hand, turned on his heel, and disappeared in an instant among the crowd.

I trust that I am not more dense than my neighbours, but I was always oppressed with a sense of my own stupidity in my dealings with Sherlock Holmes. Here I had heard what he had heard, I had seen what he had seen, and yet from his words it was evident that he saw clearly not only what had happened but what was about to happen, while to me the whole business was still confused and grotesque. As I drove home to my house in Kensington I thought over it all, from the extraordinary story of the red-headed copier of the *Encyclopaedia* down to the visit to

Saxe-Coburg Square, and the **ominous** words with which he had parted from me. What was this **nocturnal** expedition, and why should I go armed? Where were we going, and what were we to do? I had the hint from Holmes that this smooth-faced pawnbroker's assitant was a formidable man – a man who might play a deep game. I tried to puzzle it out, but gave it up in despair and set the matter aside until night should bring an explanation.

It was a quarter-past nine when I started from home and made my way across the Park, and so through Oxford Street to Baker Street. Two hansoms were standing at the door, and as I entered the passage I heard the sound of voices from above. On entering his room, I found Holmes in animated conversation with two men, one of whom I recognized as Peter Jones, the official police agent, while the other was a long, thin, sad-faced man, with a very shiny hat and oppressively respectable frock-coat.

"Ha! Our party is complete," said Holmes, buttoning up his pea-jacket and taking his heavy hunting crop from the rack. "Watson, I think you know Mr. Jones, of Scotland Yard? Let me introduce you to Mr. Merryweather, who is to be our companion in to-night's adventure."

"We're hunting in couples again, Doctor, you see," said Jones in his consequential way. "Our friend here is a wonderful man for starting a chase. All he wants is an old dog to help him to do the running down."

---

ominous: suggesting evil or harm; threatening

nocturnal: of or happening at night

"I hope a wild goose may not prove to be the end of our chase," observed Mr. Merryweather gloomily.

"You may place considerable confidence in Mr. Holmes, sir," said the police agent **loftily**. "He has his own little methods, which are, if he won't mind my saying so, just a little too theoretical and fantastic, but he has the makings of a detective in him. It is not too much to say that once or twice, as in that business of the Sholto murder and the Agra treasure, he has been more nearly correct than the official force."

"Oh, if you say so, Mr. Jones, it is all right," said the stranger with deference. "Still, I confess that I miss my rubber. It is the first Saturday night for seven-and-twenty years that I have not had my rubber."

"I think you will find," said Sherlock Holmes, "that you will play for a higher stake to-night than you have ever done yet, and that the play will be more exciting. For you, Mr. Merryweather, the stake will be some £30,000; and for you, Jones, it will be the man upon whom you wish to lay your hands."

"John Clay, the murderer, thief, smasher, and forger. He's a young man, Mr. Merryweather, but he is at the head of his profession, and I would rather have my bracelets on him than on any criminal in London. He's a remarkable man, is young John Clay. His grandfather was a royal duke, and he himself has been to Eton and Oxford. His brain is as **cunning** as his fingers, and

---

loftily: arrogantly

cunning: shrewd; tricky

though we meet signs of him at every turn, we never know where to find the man himself. He'll crack a crib in Scotland one week, and be raising money to build an orphanage in Cornwall the next. I've been on his track for years and have never set eyes on him yet."

"I hope that I may have the pleasure of introducing you to-night. I've had one or two little turns also with Mr. John Clay, and I agree with you that he is at the head of his profession. It is past ten, however, and quite time that we started. If you two will take the first hansom, Watson and I will follow in the second."

Sherlock Holmes was not very communicative during the long drive and lay back in the cab humming the tunes which he had heard in the afternoon. We rattled through an endless labyrinth of gas-lit streets until we emerged into Farrington Street.

"We are close there now," my friend remarked. "This fellow Merryweather is a bank director, and personally interested in the matter. I thought it as well to have Jones with us also. He is not a bad fellow, though an absolute **imbecile** in his profession. He has one positive virtue. He is as brave as a bulldog and as **tenacious** as a lobster if he gets his claws upon anyone. Here we are, and they are waiting for us."

We had reached the same crowded thoroughfare in which we had found ourselves in the morning. Our cabs were dismissed, and, following the guidance of Mr. Merryweather, we passed

---

imbecile: fool

tenacious: firm; unyielding

down a narrow passage and through a side door, which he opened for us. Within there was a small corridor, which ended in a very massive iron gate. This also was opened, and led down a flight of winding stone steps, which terminated at another formidable gate. Mr. Merryweather stopped to light a lantern, and then conducted us down a dark, earth-smelling passage, and so, after opening a third door, into a huge vault or cellar, which was piled all round with crates and massive boxes.

"You are not very **vulnerable** from above," Holmes remarked as he held up the lantern and gazed about him.

"Nor from below," said Mr. Merryweather, striking his stick upon the flags which lined the floor. "Why, dear me, it sounds quite hollow!" he remarked, looking up in surprise.

"I must really ask you to be a little more quiet!" said Holmes severely. "You have already **imperilled** the whole success of our expedition. Might I beg that you would have the goodness to sit down upon one of those boxes, and not to interfere?"

The solemn Mr. Merryweather perched himself upon a crate, with a very injured expression upon his face, while Holmes fell upon his knees upon the floor and, with the lantern and a magnifying lens, began to examine minutely the cracks between the stones. A few seconds sufficed to satisfy him, for he sprang to his feet again and put his glass in his pocket.

"We have at least an hour before us," he remarked, "for they can hardly take any steps until the good pawnbroker is

---

vulnerable: unsafe; at risk

imperilled: endangered

safely in bed. Then they will not lose a minute, for the sooner they do their work the longer time they will have for their escape. We are at present, Doctor – as no doubt you have divined – in the cellar of the City branch of one of the principal London banks. Mr. Merryweather is the chairman of directors, and he will explain to you that there are reasons why the more daring criminals of London should take a considerable interest in this cellar at present."

"It is our French gold," whispered the director. "We have had several warnings that an attempt might be made upon it."

"Your French gold?"

"Yes. We had occasion some months ago to strengthen our resources and borrowed for that purpose 30,000 napoleons from the Bank of France. It has become known that we have never had occasion to unpack the money, and that it is still lying in our cellar. The crate upon which I sit contains 2,000 napoleons packed between layers of lead foil. Our reserve of bullion is much larger at present than is usually kept in a single branch office, and the directors have had **misgivings** upon the subject."

"Which were very well justified," observed Holmes. "And now it is time that we arranged our little plans. I expect that within an hour matters will come to a head. In the meantime Mr. Merryweather, we must put the screen over that dark lantern."

"And sit in the dark?"

"I am afraid so. I had brought a pack of cards in my pocket, and I thought that, as we were a *partie carrée*, you might

---

misgiving(s): doubt; worry

bullion: gold or silver in bulk before coining

have your rubber after all. But I see that the enemy's preparations have gone so far that we cannot risk the presence of a light. And, first of all, we must choose our positions. These are daring men, and though we shall take them at a disadvantage, they may do us some harm unless we are careful. I shall stand behind this crate, and do you conceal yourselves behind those. Then, when I flash a light upon them, close in swiftly. If they fire, Watson, have no **compunction** about shooting them down."

I placed my revolver, cocked, upon the top of the wooden case behind which I crouched. Holmes shot the slide across the front of his lantern and left us in pitch darkness – such an absolute darkness as I have never before experienced. The smell of hot metal remained to assure us that the light was still there, ready to flash out at a moment's notice. To me, with my nerves worked up to a pitch of expectancy, there was something depressing and subduing in the sudden gloom, and in the cold dank air of the vault.

"They have but one retreat," whispered Holmes. "That is back through the house into Saxe-Coburg Square. I hope that you have done what I asked you, Jones?"

"I have an inspector and two officers waiting at the front door."

"Then we have stopped all the holes. And now we must be silent and wait."

What a time it seemed! From comparing notes afterwards it was but an hour and a quarter, yet it appeared to me that the

---

compunction: pity; regret

night must have almost gone, and the dawn be breaking above us. My limbs were weary and stiff, for I feared to change my position; yet my nerves were worked up to the highest pitch of tension, and my hearing was so acute that I could not only hear the gentle breathing of my companions, but I could distinguish the deeper, heavier in-breath of the bulky Jones from the thin, sighing note of the bank director. From my position I could look over the case in the direction of the floor. Suddenly my eyes caught the glint of a light.

At first it was but a lurid spark upon the stone pavement. Then it lengthened out until it became a yellow line, and then, without any warning or sound, a gash seemed to open and a hand appeared, a white, almost womanly hand, which felt about in the centre of the little area of light. For a minute or more the hand, with its writhing fingers, protruded out of the floor. Then it was withdrawn as suddenly as it appeared, and all was dark again save the single lurid spark which marked a chink between the stones.

Its disappearance, however, was but momentary. With a rending, tearing sound, one of the broad, white stones turned over upon its side and left a square, gaping hole, through which streamed the light of a lantern. Over the edge there peeped a clean-cut, boyish face, which looked keenly about it, and then, with a hand on either side of the aperture, drew itself shoulder-high and waist-high, until one knee rested upon the edge. In another instant he stood at the side of the hole and was hauling after him a companion, lithe and small like himself, with a pale face and a shock of very red hair.

"It's all clear," he whispered. "Have you the chisel and the bags? Great Scott! Jump, Archie, jump, and I'll swing for it!"

Sherlock Holmes had sprung out and seized the intruder by the collar. The other dived down the hole, and I heard the sound of rending cloth as Jones clutched at his skirts. The light flashed upon the barrel of a revolver, but Holmes' hunting crop came down on the man's wrist, and the pistol clinked upon the stone floor.

"It's no use, John Clay," said Holmes blandly. "You have no chance at all."

"So I see," the other answered with the utmost coolness. "I fancy that my pal is all right, though I see you have got his coat-tails."

"There are three men waiting for him at the door," said Holmes.

"Oh, indeed! You seem to have done the thing very completely. I must compliment you."

"And I you," Holmes answered. "Your red-headed idea was very new and effective."

"You'll see your pal again presently," said Jones. "He's quicker at climbing down holes than I am. Just hold out while I fix the derbies."

"I beg that you will not touch me with your filthy hands," remarked our prisoner as the handcuffs clattered upon his wrists. "You may not be aware that I have royal blood in my veins. Have the goodness, also, when you address me always to say 'sir' and 'please.' "

"All right," said Jones with a stare and a snigger. "Well,

would you please, sir, march upstairs, where we can get a cab to carry your Highness to the police-station?"

"That is better," said John Clay serenely. He made a sweeping bow to the three of us and walked quietly off in the custody of the detective.

"Really, Mr. Holmes," said Mr. Merryweather as we followed them from the cellar, "I do not know how the bank can thank you or repay you. There is no doubt that you have detected and defeated in the most complete manner one of the most determined attempts at bank robbery that have ever come within my experience."

"I have had one or two little scores of my own to settle with Mr. John Clay," said Holmes. "I have been at some small expense over this matter, which I shall expect the bank to refund, but beyond that I am amply repaid by having had an experience which is in many ways unique, and by hearing the very remarkable narrative of the Red-headed League."

"You see, Watson," he explained in the early hours of the morning as we sat over a glass of whisky and soda in Baker Street, "it was perfectly obvious from the first that the only possible object of this rather fantastic business of the advertisement of the League, and the copying of the *Encyclopaedia*, must be to get this not over-bright pawnbroker out of the way for a number of hours every day. It was a curious way of managing it, but, really, it would be difficult to suggest a better. The method was no doubt suggested to Clay's ingenious mind by the colour of his accomplice's hair. The £4 a week was a lure which must draw him, and what was it to them, who were playing for thousands? They put in the advertisement, one rogue has the temporary office, the other rogue **incites** the man to apply for it, and together they manage to secure his absence every morning in the week. From the time that I heard of the assistant having come for half wages, it was obvious to me that he had some strong motive for securing the sitation."

"But how could you guess what the motive was?"

"Had there been women in the house, I should have suspected a mere vulgar intrigue. That, however, was out of the question. The man's business was a small one, and there was nothing in his house which could account for such elaborate preparations, and such an expenditure as they were at. It must, then, be something out of the house. What could it be? I thought of the assistant's fondness for photography, and his trick of vanishing into the cellar. The cellar! There was the end of this tangled clue. Then I made inquiries as to this mysterious assistant and found that I had to deal with one of the coolest and most daring criminals in London. He was doing something in the cellar – something which took many hours a day for months on end. What could it be, once more? I could think of nothing save that he was running a tunnel to some other building.

"So far I had got when we went to visit the scene of action. I surprised you by beating upon the pavement with my stick. I was ascertaining whether the cellar stretched out in front or behind. It was not in front. Then I rang the bell, and, as I hoped,

---

incites: encourages

the assistant answered it. We have had some skirmishes, but we had never set eyes upon each other before. I hardly looked at his face. His knees were what I wished to see. You must yourself have remarked how worn, wrinkled, and stained they were. They spoke of those hours of burrowing. The only remaining point was what they were burrowing for. I walked round the corner, saw the City and Suburban Bank abutted on our friend's premises, and felt that I had solved my problem. When you drove home after the concert I called upon Scotland Yard and upon the chairman of the bank directors, with the result that you have seen."

"And how could you tell that they would make their attempt to-night?" I asked.

"Well, when they closed their League offices that was a sign that they cared no longer about Mr. Jabez Wilson's presence – in other words, that they had completed their tunnel. But it was essential that they should use it soon, as it might be discovered, or the bullion might be removed. Saturday would suit them better than any other day, as it would give them two days for their escape. For all these reasons I expected them to come to-night."

"You reasoned it out beautifully," I exclaimed in **unfeigned** admiration. "It is so long a chain, and yet every link rings true."

"It saved me from ennui," he answered, yawning. "Alas! I already feel it closing in upon me. My life is spent in one long effort to escape from the commonplaces of existence. These little

---

unfeigned: real; sincere

ennui: a feeling of dissatisfaction arising from a lack of excitement

problems help me to do so."

"And you are a benefactor of the race," said I.

He shrugged his shoulders. "Well, perhaps, after all, it is of some little use," he remarked. " '*L'homme c'est rien – l'oeuvre c'est tout*,' as Gustave Flaubert wrote to George Sand."

how did the assistant ensure that he would be hired?

L'homme c'est rien – l'oeuvre c'est tout: (French) It is not man but his work that matters.

The Open Window

3rd POV (limited)

"My aunt will be down presently, Mr. Nuttel," said a very self-possessed young lady of fifteen; "in the meantime you must try and put up with me."

Framton Nuttel **endeavoured** to say the correct something which should **duly** flatter the niece of the moment without unduly **discounting** the aunt that was to come. Privately he doubted more than ever whether these formal visits on a succession of total strangers would do much towards helping the nerve cure which he was supposed to be undergoing.

"I know how it will be," his sister had said when he was preparing to migrate to this rural **retreat**; "you will bury yourself down there and not speak to a living soul, and your nerves will be worse than ever from **moping**. I shall just give you letters of introduction to all the people I know there. Some of them, as far as I can remember, were quite nice."

Framton wondered whether Mrs. Sappleton, the lady to whom he was presenting one of the letters of introduction, came into the nice division.

---

endeavoured: made an effort

duly: properly

discounting: disregarding; ignoring

retreat: place of privacy or seclusion

moping: feeling unhappy; self-pitying

"Do you know many of the people round here?" asked the niece, when she judged that they had had sufficient silent communion.

"Hardly a soul," said Framton. "My sister was staying here, at the rectory, you know, some four years ago, and she gave me letters of introduction to some of the people here."

He made the last statement in a tone of distinct regret.

"Then you know practically nothing about my aunt?" pursued the self-possessed young lady.

"Only her name and address," admitted the caller. He was wondering whether Mrs. Sappleton was in the married or widowed state. An undefinable something about the room seemed to suggest masculine habitation.

"Her great tragedy happened just three years ago," said the child; "that would be since your sister's time."

"Her tragedy?" asked Framton; somehow in this restful country spot tragedies seemed out of place.

"You may wonder why we keep that window wide open on an October afternoon," said the niece, indicating a large French window that opened on to a lawn.

"It is quite warm for the time of the year," said Framton; "but has that window got anything to do with the tragedy?"

"Out through that window, three years ago to a day, her husband and her two young brothers went off for their day's shooting. They never came back. In crossing the moor to their

rectory: a member of the clergy's house

favourite snipe-shooting ground they were all three **engulfed** in a treacherous piece of bog. It had been that dreadful wet summer, you know, and places that were safe in other years gave way suddenly without warning. Their bodies were never recovered. That was the dreadful part of it." Here the child's voice lost its self-possessed note and became falteringly human. "Poor aunt always thinks that they will come back some day, they and the little brown spaniel that was lost with them, and walk in at that window just as they used to do. That is why the window is kept open every evening till it is quite dusk. Poor dear aunt, she has often told me how they went out, her husband with his white waterproof coat over his arm, and Ronnie, her youngest brother, singing 'Bertie, why do you bound?' as he always did to tease her, because she said it got on her nerves. Do you know, sometimes on still, quiet evenings like this, I almost get a creepy feeling that they will all walk in through that window –"

She broke off with a little shudder. It was a relief to Framton when the aunt bustled into the room with a whirl of apologies for being late in making her appearance.

"I hope Vera has been amusing you?" she said.

"She has been very interesting," said Framton.

"I hope you don't mind the open window," said Mrs. Sappleton briskly; "my husband and brothers will be home directly from shooting, and they always come in this way. They've been out for snipe in the marshes to-day, so they'll make a fine mess over my poor carpets. So like you men-folk, isn't it?"

---

engulfed: submerged; drowned

She rattled on cheerfully about the shooting and the scarcity of birds, and the prospects for duck in the winter. To Framton it was all purely horrible. He made a desperate but only partially successful effort to turn the talk on to a less **ghastly** topic; he was conscious that his hostess was giving him only a fragment of her attention, and her eyes were constantly straying past him to the open window and the lawn beyond. It was cerainly an unfortunate coincidence that he should have paid his visit on this tragic anniversary.

"The doctors agree in ordering me complete rest, an absence of mental excitement, and avoidance of anything in the nature of violent physical exercise," announced Framton, who laboured under the tolerably widespread **delusion** that toal strangers and chance acquaintances are hungry for the least detail of one's ailments and **infirmities**, their cause and cure. "On the matter of diet they are not so much in agreement," he continued.

"No?" said Mrs. Sappleton, in a voice which only replaced a yawn at the last moment. Then she suddenly brightened into alert attention – but not to what Framton was saying.

"Here they are at last!" she cried. "Just in time for tea, and don't they look as if they were muddy up to the eyes!"

Framton shivered slightly and turned towards the niece with a look intended to **convey** sympathetic comprehension. The

---

ghastly: terrible; frightful

delusion: false belief

infirmities: weaknesses

convey: make known; communicate

child was staring out through the open window with dazed horror in her eyes. In a chill shock of nameless fear Framton swung round in his seat and looked in the same direction.

In the deepening twilight three figures were walking across the lawn towards the window; they all carried guns under their arms, and one of them was additionally burdened with a white coat hung over his shoulders. A tired brown spaniel kept close at their heels. Noiselessly they neared the house, and then a hoarse young voice chanted out of the dusk: "I said, Bertie, why do you bound?"

Framton grabbed wildly at his stick and hat; the hall-door, the gravel-drive, and the front gate were dimly-noted stages in his headlong retreat. A cyclist coming along the road had to run into the hedge to avoid an **imminent** collision.

"Here we are, my dear," said the bearer of the white mackintosh, coming in through the window; "fairly muddy, but most of it's dry. Who was that who bolted out as we came up?"

"A most extraordinary man, a Mr. Nuttel," said Mrs. Sappleton; "could only talk about his illnesses, and dashed off without a word of good-bye or apology when you arrived. One would think he had seen a ghost."

"I expect it was the spaniel," said the niece calmly; "he told me he had a horror of dogs. He was once hunted into a cemetery somewhere on the banks of the Ganges by a pack of pariah dogs, and had to spend the night in a newly dug grave with the creatures snarling and grinning and foaming just above him.

---

imminent: about to take place

Enough to make anyone lose their nerve."

Romance at short notice was her speciality.

Was Vera lying? Or was she crazy?

The Faith of Men

"Tell you what we'll do; we'll shake for it."

"That suits me," said the second man, turning, as he spoke, to the Indian that was mending snowshoes in a corner of the cabin. "Here, you Billebedam, take a run down to Oleson's cabin like a good fellow, and tell him we want to borrow his dice box."

This sudden request in the midst of a council on wages of men, wood, and grub surprised Billebedam. Besides, it was early in the day, and he had never known white men of the **calibre** of Pentfield and Hutchinson to dice and play till the day's work was done. But his face was impassive as a Yukon Indian's should be, as he pulled on his mittens and went out the door.

Though eight o'clock, it was still dark outside, and the cabin was lighted by a tallow candle thrust into an empty whisky bottle. It stood on the pine-board table in the middle of a **disarray** of dirty tin dishes. Tallow from **innumerable** candles had dripped down the long neck of the bottle and hardened into a miniature glacier. The small room, which composed the entire cabin, was as badly littered as the table; while at one end, against the wall, were two bunks, one above the other, with the blankets turned down just as the two men had crawled out in the morning.

---

calibre: character; quality

disarray: disorder

innumerable: too many; countless

Lawrence Pentfield and Corry Hutchinson were millionaires, though they did not look it. There seemed nothing unusual about them, while they would have passed muster as fair specimens of lumbermen in any Michigan camp. But outside, in the darkness, where holes yawned in the ground, were many men engaged in windlassing muck and gravel and gold from the bottoms of the holes where other men received fifteen dollars per day for scraping it from off the bedrock. Each day thousands of dollars' worth of gold were scraped from bedrock and windlassed to the surface, and it all belonged to Pentfield and Hutchinson, who took their rank among the richest kings of Bonanza.

Pentfield broke the silence that followed on Billebedam's departure by heaping the dirty plates higher on the table and drumming a tattoo on the cleared space with his knuckles. Hutchinson snuffed the smoky candle and reflectively rubbed the soot from the wick between thumb and forefinger.

"By Jove, I wish we could both go out!" he abruptly exclaimed. "That would settle it all."

Pentfield looked at him darkly.

"If it weren't for your cursed obstinacy, it'd be settled anyway. All you have to do is get up and go. I'll look after things, and next year I can go out."

"Why should I go? I've no one waiting for me –"

"Your people," Pentfield broke in roughly.

"Like you have," Hutchinson went on. "A girl, I mean, and you know it."

Pentfield shrugged his shoulders gloomily. "She can wait, I

guess."

"But she's been waiting two years now."

"And another won't age her beyond recognition."

"That'd be three years. Think of it, old man, three years in this end of the earth, this falling-off place for the damned!" Hutchinson threw up his arm in an almost **articulate** groan.

He was several years younger than his partner, not more than twenty-six, and there was a certain **wistfulness** in his face that comes into the faces of men when they yearn vainly for the things they have been long denied. This same wistfulness was in Pentfield's face, and the groan of it was articulate in the heave of his shoulders.

"I dreamed last night I was in Zinkand's," he said. "The music playing, glasses clinking, voices humming, women laughing, and I was ordering eggs – yes, sir, eggs, fried and boiled and poached and scrambled, and in all sorts of ways, and downing them as fast as they arrived."

"I'd have ordered salads and green things," Hutchinson criticized hungrily, "with a big, rare, Porterhouse, and young onions and radishes, - the kind your teeth sink into with a crunch."

"I'd have followed the eggs with them, I guess, if I hadn't awakened," Pentfield replied.

He picked up a trail-scarred banjo from the floor and began

---

articulate: clear

wistfulness: longing

to strum a few wandering notes. Hutchinson **winced** and breathed heavily.

"Quit it!" he burst out with sudden fury, as the other struck into a gaily lifting swing. "It drives me mad. I can't stand it."

Pentfield tossed the banjo into a bunk and quoted:-

"Hear me babble what the weakest won't confess-

I am Memory and Torment – I am Town!

I am all that ever went with evening dress!"

The other man winced where he sat and dropped his head forward on the table. Pentfield **resumed** the **monotonous** drumming with his knuckles. A loud snap from the door attracted his attention. The frost was creeping up the inside in a white sheet, and he began to hum:-

"The flocks are folded, boughs are bare,

The salmon takes the sea;

And oh, my fair, would I somewhere

Might house my heart with thee."

Silence fell and was not again broken till Billebedam arrived and threw the dice box on the table.

"Um much cold," he said. "Oleson um speak to me, um say um Yukon freeze last night."

"Hear that, old man!" Pentfield cried, slapping Hutchinson on the shoulder. "Whoever wins can be hitting the trail for God's country this time tomorrow morning!"

---

winced: showed distress with a facial expression

resumed: continued

monotonous: unchanging and boring

gaily: in a cheerful way

He picked up the box, **briskly** rattling the dice.

"What'll it be?"

"Straight poker dice," Hutchinson answered. "Go on and roll them out."

Pentfield swept the dishes from the table with a crash and rolled out the five dice. Both looked tragedy. The shake was without a pair and five-spot high.

"A stiff!" Pentfield groaned.

After much **deliberating** Pentfield picked up all the five dice and put them in the box.

"I'd shake to the five if I were you," Hutchinson suggested.

"No, you wouldn't, not when you see this," Pentfield replied, shaking out the dice.

Again they were without a pair, running this time in unbroken sequence from two to six.

"A second stiff!" he groaned. "No use your shaking, Corry. You can't lose."

The other man gathered up the dice without a word, rattled them, rolled them out on the table with a flourish, and saw that he had likewise shaken a six-high stiff.

"Tied you, anyway, but I'll have to do better than that," he said, gathering in four of them and shaking to the six. "And here's what beats you!"

But they rolled out deuce, tray, four, and five – a stiff still and no better nor worse than Pentfield's throw.

---

briskly: quickly

deliberating: careful thought; consideration

Hutchinson sighed.

"Couldn't happen once in a million times," he said.

"Nor in a million lives," Pentfield added, catching up the dice and quickly throwing them out. Three fives appeared, and, after much delay, he was rewarded by a fourth five on the second shake. Hutchinson seemed to have lost his last hope.

But three sixes turned up on his first shake. A great doubt rose in the other's eyes, and hope returned into his. He had one more shake. Another six and he would go over the ice to salt water and the States.

He rattled the dice in the box, made as though to cast them, hesitated, and continued to rattle them.

"Go on! Go on! Don't take all night about it!" Pentfield cried sharply, bending his nails on the table, so tight was the clutch with which he strove to control himself.

The dice rolled forth, an upturned six meeting their eyes. Both men sat staring at it. There was a long silence. Hutchinson shot a **covert** glance at his partner, who, still more covertly, caught it, and pursed up his lips in an attempt to advertise his unconcern.

Hutchinson laughed as he got up on his feet. It was a nervous, **apprehensive** laugh. It was a case where it was more awkward to win than lose. He walked over to his partner, who whirled upon him fiercely:-

"Now you just shut up, Corry! I know all you're going to

---

covert: secret

apprehensive: anxious

say – that you'd rather stay in and let me go, and all that; so don't say it. You've your own people in Detroit to see, and that's enough. Besides, you can do for me the very thing I expected to do if I went out."

"And that is - ?"

Pentfield read the full question in his partner's eyes, and answered:-

"Yes, that very thing. You can bring her in to me. The only difference will be a Dawson wedding instead of a San Franciscan one."

"But, man alike!" Corry Hutchinson objected. "How under the sun can I bring her in? We're not exactly brother and sister, seeing that I have not even met her, and it wouldn't be just the proper thing, you know, for us to travel together. Of course, it would be all right – you and I know that; but think of the looks of it, man!"

Pentfield swore under his breath, consigning the looks of it to a less frigid region than Alaska.

"Now, if you'll just listen and not get astride that high horse of yours so blamed quick," his partner went on, "you'll see that the only fair thing under the circumstances is for me to let you go out this year. Next year is only a year away, and then I can take my fling."

Pentfield shook his head, though visibly swayed by the temptation.

"It won't do, Corry, old man. I appreciate your kindness and all that, but it won't do. I'd be ashamed every time I thought of you slaving away in here in my place."

A thought seemed suddenly to strike him. Burrowing into his bunk and disrupting it in his eagerness, he secured a writing-pad and pencil, and sitting down at the table, began to write with swiftness and certitude.

"Here," he said, thrusting the scrawled letter into his partner's hand. "You just deliver that and everything'll be all right."

Hutchinson ran his eye over it and laid it down.

"How do you know the brother will be willing to make that beastly trip in here?" he demanded.

"Oh, he'll do it for me – and for his sister," Pentfield replied. "You see, he's tenderfoot, and I wouldn't trust her with him alone. But with you along it will be an easy trip and a safe one. As soon as you get out, you'll go to her and prepare her. Then you can take your run east to your own people, and in the spring she and her brother'll be ready to start with you. You'll like her, I know, right from the jump; and from that, you'll know her as soon as you lay eyes on her."

So saying he opened the back of his watch and exposed a girl's photograph pasted on the inside of the case. Corry Hutchinson gazed at it with admiration welling up in his eyes.

"Mabel is her name," Pentfield went on. "And it's just as well you should know how to find the house. Soon as you strike 'Frisco, take a cab, and just say, 'Holmes's place, Myrdon Avenue' – I doubt if the Myrdon Avenue is necessary. The cabby'll know where Judge Holmes lives."

"And say," Pentfield continued, after a pause, "it won't be a bad idea for you to get me a few things which a – er –"

"A married man should have in his business," Hutchinson blurted out with a grin.

Pentfield grinned back.

"Sure, napkins and tablecloths and sheets and pillowslips, and such things. And you might get a good set of china. You know it'll come hard for her to settle down to this sort of thing. You can freight them in by steamer around by Bering Sea. And, I say, what's the matter with a piano?"

Hutchinson seconded the idea heartily. His reluctance had **vanished**, and he was warming up to his mission.

"By Jove! Lawrence," he said at the conclusion of the council, as they both rose to their feet, "I'll bring back that girl of yours in style. I'll do the cooking and take care of the dogs, and all that brother'll have to do will be to see to her comfort and do for her whatever I've forgotten. And I'll forget damn little, I can tell you."

The next day Lawrence Pentfield shook hands with him for the last time and watched him, running with his dogs, disappear up the frozen Yukon on his way to salt water and the world. Pentfield went back to his Bonanza mine, which was many times more **dreary** than before, and faced **resolutely** into the long winter. There was work to be done, men to superintend, and operations to direct in burrowing after the erratic pay streak; but his heart was not in the work. Nor was his heart in any work till

---

vanished: disappeared

dreary: dull

resolutely: with determination

the tiered logs of a new cabin began to rise on the hill behind the mine. It was a grand cabin, warmly built and divided into three comfortable rooms. Each log was hand-hewed and squared – an expensive **whim** when the axemen received a daily wage of fifteen dollars; but to him nothing could be too costly for the home in which Mabel Holmes was to live.

So he went about with the building of the cabin, singing, "And oh, my fair, would I somewhere might house my heart with thee!" Also, he had a calender pinned on the wall above the table, and his first act each morning was to check off the day and to count the days that were left ere his partner would come booming down the Yukon ice in the spring. Another whim of his was to permit no one to sleep in the new cabin on the hill. It must be as fresh for her occupancy as the square-hewed wood was fresh; and when it stood complete, he put a padlock on the door. No one entered save himself, and he was wont to spend long hours there, and to come forth with his face strangely radiant and in his eyes a glad, warm light.

In December he received a letter from Corry Hutchinson. He had just seen Mabel Holmes. She was all she ought to be, to be Lawrence Pentfield's wife, he wrote. He was enthusiastic, and his letter sent the blood tingling through Pentfield's veins. Other letters followed, one on the heels of another, and sometimes two or three together when the mail lumped up. And they were all in the same tenor. Corry had just come from Myrdon Avenue; Corry was just going to Myrdon Avenue; or Corry was at

---

whim: fancy; unusual desire

ere : before

Myrdon Avenue. And he **lingered** on and on in San Francisco, nor even mentioned his trip to Detroit.

Lawrence Pentfield began to think that his partner was a great deal in the company of Mabel Holmes for a fellow who was going east to see his people. He even caught himself worrying about it at times, though he would have worried more had he not known Mabel and Corry so well. Mabel's letters, on the other hand, had a great deal to say about Corry. Also, a thread of timidity that was near to disinclination ran through them concerning the trip in over the ice and the Dawson marriage. Pentfield wrote back heartily, laughing at her fears, which he took to be the mere physical ones of danger and hardship rather than those bred of maidenly reserve.

But the long winter and **tedious** wait, following upon the two previous long winters, were telling upon him. The superintendence of the men and the pursuit of the pay streak could not break the irk of the daily round, and the end of January found him making occasional trips to Dawson, where he could forget his identity for a space at the gambling tables. Because he could afford to lose, he won, and 'Pentfield's luck' became a stock phrase among the faro players.

His luck ran with him till the second week in February. How much farther it might have run is conjectural; for, after one big game, he never played again.

It was in the Opera House that it occurred, and for an hour it

---

lingered: remained

tedious: boring

had seemed that he could not place his money on a card without making the card a winner. In the lull at the end of a deal, while the game-keeper was shuffling the deck, Nick Inwood, the owner of the game, remarked, apropos of nothing:-

"I say, Pentfield, I see that partner of yours has been cutting up monkey-shines on the outside."

"Trust Corry to have a good time," Pentfield had answered; "especially when he has earned it."

"Every man to his taste," Nick Inwood laughed; "but I should scarcely call getting married a good time."

"Corry married!" Pentfield cried, incredulous and yet surprised out of himself for the moment.

"Sure," Inwood said. "I saw it in the 'Frisco paper that came in over the ice this morning."

"Well, and who's the girl?" Pentfield demanded, somewhat with the air of patient fortitude with which one takes the bait of a catch and is aware at the time of the large laugh bound to follow at his expense.

Nick Inwood pulled the newspaper from his pocket and began looking it over, saying:-

"I haven't a remarkable memory for names, but it seems to me it's something like Mabel – Mabel – oh yes, here is it – 'Mabel Holmes, daughter of Judge Holmes,' – whoever he is."

Lawrence Pentfield never turned a hair, though he wondered how any man in the North could know her name. He glanced coolly from face to face to note any vagrant signs of the game that was being played upon him, but beyond a healthy curiosity the faces betrayed nothing. Then he turned to the gambler and

apropos: with reference to

said in cold, even tones:-

"Inwood, I've got an even five hundred here that says the print of what you have just said is not in that paper."

The gambler looked at him in **quizzical** surprise. "Go 'way, child. I don't want your money."

"I thought so," Pentfield sneered, returning to the game and laying a couple of bets.

Nick Inwood's face flushed, and, as though doubting his senses, he ran careful eyes over the print of a quarter of a column. Then he turned on Lawrence Pentfield.

"Look here, Pentfield," he said, in a quiet, nervous manner; "I can't allow that, you know."

"Allow what?" Pentfield demanded brutally.

"You implied that I lied."

"Nothing of the sort," came the reply. "I merely implied that you were trying to be clumsily witty."

"Make your bets, gentlemen," the dealer protested.

"But I tell you it's true," Nick Inwood insisted.

"And I have told you I've five hundred that says it's not in that paper," Pentfield answered, at the same time throwing a heavy sack of dust on the table.

"I am sorry to take your money," was the retort, as Inwood thrust the newspaper into Pentfield's hand.

Pentfield saw, though he could not quite bring himself to believe. Glancing through the headline, 'Young Lochinvar came out of the North,' and skimming the article until the names of

---

quizzical: questioning

Mabel Holmes and Corry Hutchinson, coupled together, leaped squarely before his eyes, he turned to the top of the page. It was a San Francisco paper.

"The money's yours, Inwood," he remarked, with a short laugh. "There's no telling what that partner of mine will do when he gets started."

Then he returned to the article and read it word for word, very slowly and very carefully. He could no longer doubt. Beyond dispute, Corry Hutchinson had married Mabel Holmes. 'One of the Bonanza kings,' it described him, 'a partner with Lawrence Pentfield (whom San Francisco society has not yet forgotten), and interested with that gentleman in other rich, Klondike properties.' Further, and at the end, he read, 'It is whispered that Mr. and Mrs. Hutchinson will, after a brief trip east to Detroit, make their real honeymoon journey into the fascinating Klondike country.'

"I'll be back again; keep my place for me," Pentfield said, rising to his feet and taking his sack, which meantime had hit the blower and came back lighter by five hundred dollars.

He went down the street and bought a Seattle paper. It contained the same facts, though somewhat condensed. Corry and Mabel were indubitably married. Pentfield returned to the Opera House and resumed his seat in the game. He asked to have the limit removed.

"Trying to get action," Nick Inwood laughed, as he nodded assent to the dealer. "I was going down to the A. C. store, but now I guess I'll stay and watch you do your worst."

This Lawrence Pentfield did at the end of two hours'

plunging, when the dealer bit the end off a fresh cigar and struck a match as he announced that the bank was broken. Pentfield cashed in for forty thousand, shook hands with Nick Inwood, and stated that it was the last time he would ever play at his game or at anybody else's.

No one knew nor guessed that he had been hit, much less hit hard. There was no apparent change in his manner. For a week he went about his work much as he had always done, when he read an account of the marriage in a Portland paper. Then he called in a friend to take charge of his mine and departed up the Yukon behind his dogs. He held to the Salt Water trail till White River was reached, into which he turned. Five days later he came upon a hunting camp of the White River Indians. In the evening there was a feast, and he sat in honour beside the chief; and next morning he headed his dogs back toward the Yukon. But he no longer travelled alone. A young squaw fed his dogs for him that night and helped to pitch camp. She had been mauled by a bear in her childhood and suffered from a slight limp. Her name was Lashka, and she was **diffident** at first with the strange white man that had come out of the Unknown, married her with scarcely a look or word, and now was carrying her back with him into the Unknown.

But Lashka's was better fortune than falls to most Indian girls that mate with white men in the Northland. No sooner was Dawson reached than the barbaric marriage that had joined them was re-solemnized, in the white man's fashion, before a priest.

---

diffident: shy; insecure

From Dawson, which to her was all a marvel and a dream, she was taken directly to the Bonanza claim and installed in the square-hewed cabin on the hill.

The nine days' wonder that followed arose not so much out of the fact of the squaw whom Lawrence Pentfield had taken to bed and board as out of the ceremony that had legalized the tie. The properly sanctioned marriage was the one thing that passed the community's comprehension. But no one bothered Pentfield about it. So long as a man's vagaries did no special hurt to the community, the community let the man alone, nor was Pentfield barred from the cabins of men who possessed white wives. The marriage ceremony removed him from the status of squaw-man and placed him beyond moral reproach, though there were men that challenged his taste where women were concerned.

No more letters arrived from the outside. Six sledloads of mails had been lost at the Big Salmon. Besides, Pentfield knew that Corry and his bride must by that time have started in over the trail. They were even then on their honeymoon trip – the honeymoon trip he had dreamed of for himself through two dreary years. His lip curled with bitterness at the thought; but beyond being kinder to Lashka he gave no sign.

March had passed and April was nearing its end, when, one spring morning, Lashka asked permission to go down the creek several miles to Siwash Pete's cabin. Pete's wife, a Stewart River woman, had sent up word that something was wrong with her baby, and Lashka, who was pre-eminently a mother-woman and who held herself to be truly wise in the matter of infantile troubles, missed no opportunity of nursing the children of other women as yet more fortunate than she.

Pentfield harnessed his dogs, and with Lashka behind took the trail down the creek bed of Bonanza. Spring was in the air. The sharpness had gone out of the bite of the frost and though snow still covered the land, the murmur and trickling of water told that the iron grip of winter was relaxing. The bottom was dropping out of the trail, and here and there a new trail had been broken around open holes. At such a place, where there was not room for two sleds to pass, Pentfield heard the jingle of approaching bells and stopped his dogs.

A team of tired-looking dogs appeared around the narrow bend, followed by a heavily-loaded sled. At the gee-pole was a man who steered in a manner familiar to Pentfield, and behind the sled walked two women. His glance returned to the man at the gee-pole. It was Corry. Pentfield got on his feet and waited. He was glad that Lashka was with him. The meeting could not have come about better had it been planned, he thought. And as he waited he wondered what they would say, what they would be able to say. As for himself there was no need to say anything. The explaining was all on their side, and he was ready to listen to them.

As they drew in abreast, Corry recognized him and halted the dogs. With a "Hello, old man," he held out his hand.

Pentfield shook it, but without warmth or speech. By this time the two women had come up, and he noticed that the second one was Dora Holmes. He doffed his fur cap, the flaps of which were flying, shook hands with her, and turned toward Mabel. She swayed forward, splendid and radiant, but faltered before his outstretched hand. He had intended to say, "How do you do, Mrs. Hutchinson?" – but somehow, the Mrs. Hutchinson had choked him, and all he had managed to articulate was the "How do you do?"

There was all the constraint and awkwardness in the situation he could have wished. Mabel betrayed the agitation appropriate to her position, while Dora, evidently brought along as some sort of peacemaker, was saying:-

"Why, what is the matter, Lawrence?"

Before he could answer, Corry plucked him by the sleeve and drew him aside.

"See here, old man, what's this mean?" Corry demanded in a low tone, indicating Lashka with his eyes.

"I can hardly see, Corry, where you can have any concern in the matter," Pentfield answered mockingly.

But Corry drove straight to the point.

"What is that squaw doing on your sled? A nasty job you've given me to explain all this away. I only hope it can be explained away. Who is she? Whose squaw is she?"

Then Lawrence Pentfield delivered his stroke, and he delivered it with a certain calm elation of spirit that seemed somewhat to **compensate** for the wrong that had been done him.

"She is my squaw," he said; "Mrs. Pentfield, if you please."

Corry Hutchinson gasped, and Pentfield left him and returned to the two women. Mabel, with a worried expression on

---

compensate: make up for

her face, seemed holding herself **aloof**. He turned to Dora and asked, quite genially, as though all the world was sunshine: - "How did you stand the trip, anyway? Have any trouble to sleep warm?"

"And, how did Mrs. Hutchinson stand it?" he asked next, his eyes on Mabel.

"Oh, you dear ninny!" Dora cried, throwing her arms around him and hugging him. "Then you saw it, too! I thought something was the matter, you were acting so strangely."

"I – I hardly understand," he stammered.

"It was corrected in next day's paper," Dora chattered on. "We did not dream you would see it. All the other papers had it correctly, and of course that one miserable paper was the very one you saw!"

"Wait a moment! What do you mean?" Pentfield demanded, a sudden fear at his heart, for he felt himself on the verge of a great gulf.

But Dora swept volubly on.

"Why, when it became known that Mabel and I were going to Klondike, *Every Other Week* said that when we were gone, it would be lovely on Myrdon Avenue, meaning of course, lonely."

"Then – "

"I am Mrs. Hutchinson," Dora answered. "And you thought it was Mabel all the time – "

"Precisely the way of it," Pentfield replied slowly. "But I can see now. The reporter got the names mixed. The Seattle and

---

aloof: distant

Portland paper copied."

He stood silently for a minute. Mabel's face was turned toward him again, and he could see the glow of expectancy in it. Corry was deeply interested in the ragged toe of one of his moccasins, while Dora was stealing sidelong glances at the immobile face of Lashka sitting on the sled. Lawrence Pentfield stared straight out before him into a dreary future, through the grey vistas of which he saw himself riding on a sled behind running dogs with lame Lashka by his side.

Then he spoke, quite simply, looking Mabel in the eyes.

"I am very sorry. I did not dream it. I thought you had married Corry. That is Mrs. Pentfield sitting on the sled over there."

Mabel Holmes turned weakly toward her sister, as though all the fatigue of her great journey had suddenly descended on her. Dora caught her around the waist. Corry Hutchinson was still occupied with his moccasins. Pentfield glanced quickly from face to face, then turned to his sled.

"Can't stop here all day, with Pete's baby waiting," he said to Lashka.

The long whip-lash hissed out, the dogs sprang against the breast bands, and the sled lurched and jerked ahead.

"Oh, I say, Corry," Pentfield called back, "you'd better occupy the old cabin. It's not been used for some time. I've built a new one on the hill."

Don't make desisions without Knowing all the facts.

Why couldn't P go w/ H?

Made in the USA
Middletown, DE
29 June 2023

34199321R00086